Jake, The Y Farmer's Laa

A Gay Historical Erotic Journey Of Discovery

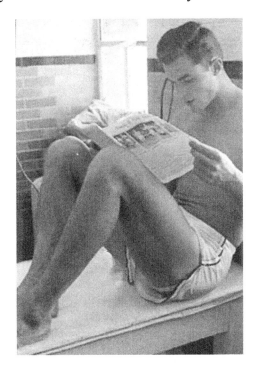

Joey Jenkinson

DbBooks

Joey says:
This is a historical drama, set in England during the 1960s, at a time when there was no such thing as safe sex between gay men, a pre-AIDS era when condoms were only used as a means of preventing pregnancy and sexually transmitted diseases.

1: The Storm House

June 1964

For two years, since his mother's suicide, Jake Nelson had been looking for an excuse to leave Partridge Farm. Now he believed he had found one. Two months ago his equally long-suffering brothers—25-year-old Paul and 23-year-old Pete—had gone off to Australia, as "Ten-Pound Poms". It had either been that, Paul said, or doing a life sentence for killing their old man, who they held responsible for their mother's death because of the way he had treated her.

Four months ago, Eddie Nelson had been caught in "a compromising position" in the tractor shed with an 18-year-old girl from the village. Instead of calling the police—not the sort of thing you did in rural communities such as Brodsworthy, the girl's father had waylaid Eddie on his way home across the fields from the pub. He had given him a thrashing, cracking three ribs. The next day, Paul and Pete had driven into town in Eddie's Thames Trader and filled in their forms for the Assisted Passage Migration Scheme. Last week, Jake had received a letter from Paul, saying that he and Pete had found work on a sheep farm, adding that he would be guaranteed a job here, should he decide to leave Partridge Farm.

Jake *wanted* to join his brothers and get away from his obnoxious father, but short of stowing away on the ship this would be impossible. At twenty, in the eyes of the law he was still a minor, effectively still under Eddie's control.

When Eddie Nelson overheard Jake telling one of the farmhands that he was thinking of applying to the APMS so that he could join his brothers—in five months' time when he turned twenty-one, he strode up to him, cuffed him about the head and barked, "You'll do no such thing. When you turn twenty-one, you can do as you like. Until then you'll work for me and you'll do as I say. Otherwise the only way you'll be leaving this farm will be in a box."

Jake was a "war baby", born in November 1943 when times had been tough. As a child he had been sickly and a magnet for every ailment going. His mother had once told him that on two occasions, he had been *so* sickly that the doctor had warned her that he might not survive infancy. How wrong they had been! From the age of twelve, Jake had started to fill out, and he was certainly no weakling now. He was six-feet tall, and tipped the scales at a very robust 180 pounds. Most mornings—evenings too, when he could—he worked out with weights in the barn. He was as strong as a horse, and bigger than his father, but he had always been afraid of Eddie—afraid that unless he toed the line, Eddie would kick him out of the house, as he had persistently threatened to do with Paul and Pete, until they had left of their own accord.

The general feeling in the village—Pete had called it "mother's milk prejudice"—was that the apple rarely fell far from the tree, and that if Eddie was a stinker, then his sons would be the same. Nothing could have been further from the truth.

"I have to stick it out until November," Jake had told his

friend, Mark. "Where would I go if he turfed me out? The relatives think all us Nelsons shit in the same pot."

Mark Noble had been Eddie Nelson's foreman for the past eighteen months. He hated him, but tolerated him because, though he was an utter bastard, he paid his employees more than Jack Smart at the farm in the next village, his only way of holding on to them.

"You could lodge with me," Mark had told him. "Then again, that'd make things awkward because the old twat would sack me and we'd all end up sailing down the river."

Mark was thirty, a ruggedly handsome hulk of a man, with a permanent five o'clock shadow, and for whom no task was ever too tough. The villagers considered him a foreigner because he had arrived here two years ago from London and spoke with a "funny" accent. Why he had come all this way nobody seemed to know, but one rumour was that he had been the lover of a wealthy older woman in the capital, and that she had died and left him her money. The locals figured it must have been a tidy sum because when he had bought Mill Cottage—the tiny property in the dip between Partridge Farm and the lane leading up to the village—he had paid the previous owner cash-in-hand. There was also speculation as to why he lived alone.

"A blind man can see why," Eddie Nelson had told Bob, the landlord at the Cock & Crown. "Whoever she was, he had something to do with her snuffing it, and he came up here so he wouldn't get caught. But I'm not bothered. So long as he puts in a good day's work he could have killed half the royal family for all I care."

Bob had expressed an opinion of his own—that Mark and Eddie's son Jake were spending a lot of time together, and in his opinion Eddie should have been worried that some of Mark's bad habits, whatever these might have be, might rub off on Jake.

"Naw," Eddie had laughed. "The lad's too busy chasing after skirt to be influenced by what Mark might have to say. I'm not bothered about that, either, so long as he doesn't get one of his floozies in the club."

Jake was not behind the door when it came to sex. An early developer, he had begun wanking at thirteen, and had his first woman on his eighteenth birthday—an unplanned event when his brothers had taken him to the Cock & Crown to buy him his first legal pint. Paul had headed home after closing time because he had to be up at the crack of dawn to fetch the cows in from the field and do the milking but Pete had hung around waiting for the barmaid, Josie, to finish wiping the tables and washing the glasses.

Pete and Josie had been courting for six months, and Eddie Nelson had denounced her as a trollop who would go after anything with trousers. Jake had found this to be true when Pete had suddenly complained of feeling unwell, and rushed off to the toilets in the pub yard. Five minutes later he had rejoined Jake and Josie, his face as white a sheet.

"I'm off home and straight to bed," Paul had groaned to Jake. "Do us a favour and take care of Josie, will you? Here—you'll be needing this."

Pete had handed Jake a three-pack of Durex, and Josie had grabbed his hand and led him into the alleyway that ran down one side of the pub. Jake's first time had been pretty pedestrian, but good. Josie had unzipped him, taken out his cock and muttered something about him being *much* bigger than Pete, and he had gritted his teeth as she had rolled the johnny over his thick, hard shaft. Then she had raised her skirt, and Jake had not been shocked, given what he had heard about her, to observe that she had not been wearing panties. A moment later he had pushed his cock inside her, making her squeal like a stuck pig, and it had lasted a good deal longer than either of them had expected.

The next morning, Pete had given Jake the third degree. Had he fingered Josie and gone down on her first to get her wet? Had he managed to get the johnny on before shooting his load, as had happened with him the first time? Had she asked him to give it her from behind, the way she liked it? And why was there only one Durex left in the packet? Jake had told his brother nothing, only that he had done Josie twice, and he had not seen her again after that night. He had seen other women though—more in the last two years than most men would ever dream of bedding in a lifetime.

But this afternoon—and the incident in the turnip field—had put Jake in such a quandary, to such an extent that he realised his life would never be the same again.

Eddie had driven the Thames Trader into Doncaster to pick up supplies, and would not be back until tea-time. Jake was happiest when Eddie was not around, barking orders like a stocky sergeant major. He and Mark had hit it off straight away—the worldly Londoner and the timid youth that Jake had been eighteen months ago, picked on day and night by his father and once showing up with a big bruise down one side of his face that he swore had come from walking into the door-jamb after having one too many at the Cock & Crown. It had not taken Mark long to work out where that bruise had come from.

Mark had often considered tackling Eddie about the way he treated his son. He had been the same with Paul and Pete until they had stood up to him. Jake was not made that way. He was a big lad, but sensitive. He needed someone to confide in, a shoulder to lean on, and a sympathetic ear. For the past eighteen months, Mark had been that someone.

This morning when Jake came downstairs to breakfast, he found Eddie in a fouler mood than usual—sitting at the table, grizzle-faced and rheumy-eyed, and with what little hair he had looking like it had not been washed for months. The postman had been and he had seen the letter addressed to Jake, and the logo on the envelope—that of the Assisted Passage Migration Scheme.

"Don't tell me you're still on with that nonsense," Eddie growled. "If I've told you once, I've told you a thousand times. When you turn twenty-one you can do as you bloody well like, and good riddance. Until then…"

Jake did not allow him to finish. Grabbing two slices of bacon from his plate, he slapped them between two slices of bread and left the house. Five minutes later he joined Mark in the top field, to make a start on the hoeing between the turnips. And for the next hour be barely said a word.

"Girl trouble?" Mark eventually drawled, unable to cope with seeing his friend looking so perplexed.

Jake half-smiled and said, "It wouldn't be so bad if there *was* a girl. God, I can't wait for the next five months to be over. Then I'll be on my way to wherever, and hopefully never seeing this bloody place again."

"And I'd miss you terribly," Mark could not help saying, pausing to wipe the sweat from his brow.

It was only ten, and the sun was already high in the sky indicating that today would be another scorcher. Standing up and straightening his back, Mark let go of his hoe and pulled his T-shirt over his head. His broad, muscular chest was covered with a carpet of dark brown bristles, and the sudden sight of this caused Jake to catch his breath, to such an extent that Mark heard him.

"You all right, Jake?"

For a few seconds, Jake was in a trance. He felt a tingling in the pit of his stomach, the same sensation that occurred each time he saw a woman naked for the first time. Only this was *not* a woman, it was his friend, using his T-shirt to wipe the sweat from under his arms.

"It's the heat," he said. "I think we should take a break."

Mark chuckled to himself. Without meaning to, he had got his friend hot and bothered! He had always been fond of the lad, but had never thought about him in any other way but as a mate...until now. How many women was Jake said to have bedded in the community—ten, twenty? Now, he had his doubts. Why should this chirpy young lothario get all flustered because he had taken off his top? Was Jake secretly what they called a double-edged blade, one which cut both ways? And what would be the risks of finding out?

9

Dipping into his knapsack he fished out a bottle of Tizer and Jake followed him to the edge of the field, where an old oak provided them respite from the fierce summer sun.

For ten minutes they lay with their backs against the tree trunk, swigging Tizer, passing the bottle back and forth. Mark was hoping Jake might take off his T-shirt, soaked through with sweat, and which would have at least revealed that he *may* have been interested, but he kept it on.

"Seeing anyone at the moment, Jake?" he asked, for the want of something to say, when only minutes ago Jake had told him that he was not.

Jake smiled and replied, "Yes, dozens of rows of bloody turnips which aren't going to hoe themselves."

Mark grinned back, and lurched to his feet.

"You're right," he drawled. "Might as well have a piss before we get started, though."

Walking a few feet from the tree, and not bothering to turn his back, Mark unbuttoned his trousers and took out his cock, well aware that Jake was watching out of the corner of his eye. Working his foreskin back and forth a few times to get himself a little harder—but not too hard so that he was unable to pee—he arched a golden stream high into the air while whistling a few bars of "You're My World", that summer's big hit. Then after shaking off the droplets, he put his cock away and picked up his hoe.

*

That night, Jake was unable to sleep. It was humid, and his

room oppressive even though the window was open. He had bolted the door and was lying naked on top of the bed, rock-hard and in need of release. Closing his eyes, he tried to conjure up an image of the last woman he'd had sex with—Margaret Evans, who came to the farm twice a week to buy eggs for the village shop. Jake had not expected her to invite him to get into the back of her van, and he had told her that he didn't have a johnny. Margaret had told him not to worry, and at the last minute he had pulled out of her and blown his load across the trays of eggs.

Now, he closed his eyes tried to imagine that Margaret was with him on the bed, that it was not his fingers that were wrapped around his rigid log, but that it was deeply embedded in her tight, moist pussy. All he could think of, however, when he began stroking was that sweat-streaked hairy chest—of how he had wanted to caress the wealth of dark brown bristles. He could not recall what Mark's cock had looked like…only that chest! And it was while he was fantasising about shooting his jizz across that dusky carpet that he arched his back and spurted it across his abs.

*

Mark too had spent a restless night, thinking only about the young man with the black wavy hair and ever-ready smile, the eyes blue as the afternoon's cloudless sky, those full and kissable lips—and about the *big* mistake he assumed he had made, coming on to Jake the way he had in the turnip field, waving his cock at him, and all to no avail.

11

"I could have ended up looking like a fool," he muttered to himself as he set off up the hill towards the farm. "Jake's had every available woman in the village by all accounts, and the ones he hasn't had are either dried up or lezzies. Then I ask him if he's seeing anybody. I'm lucky he didn't clock me one. He's never going to want to talk to me again. And if he's blabbed about me to Eddie, I'll be out of a job."

He found Jake in the Storm House. This was a formerly derelict building that Eddie Nelson had patched up with the intention of using it as a granary, but which for some reason had fallen back into disrepair and now served as a roost for the old fowls Eddie had grown too fond of for them to end their days in the cooking pot. The upper floor was reached by a rickety ladder, and Jake had come here to check on one of his bantams that was brooding a clutch of eggs—and for a wank because, since knocking out a load last night, his hard-on had refused to go down.

"What are you doing up here?" he asked Mark, perhaps a little too brusquely.

Mark risked pointing to the big bulge in Jake's denims, then at his own.

"Great minds think alike, I suppose. I take it your latest piece didn't put out last night?"

"Red flags week," Jake responded. "How about you?"

"Something like that," Mark said, realising at once that he really *was* on to a hiding for nothing with this man, but in a devilish enough mood to at least try and get *something* out of the situation without making it too obvious.

Flopping on to a pile of straw, he took a battered pack of

Woodbines out of the pocket of his cowboy-check shirt, and handed one to Jake, who flopped down beside him.

"My mother called these coffin nails." Jake said. "The old man'll go crackers if he catches us smoking up here."

"What he doesn't see he won't know," Mark shot back. "He's gone into town. Said he won't be back until late. Do you reckon he's got a fancy-woman?"

"God help her if he has," Jake quipped, lighting up.

For ten minutes they lay back in the straw, smoking and contemplating—Mark anxious to make a move on Jake but afraid of taking the risk, Jake wanting to do the same but refraining for the same reason. His thoughts wandered back to Harry Parkin, who had been in his class during his last year at school. Effeminate had not even begun to describe Harry and one of the other boys—butch as a bull but "one of them"—had made a move on him, and ended losing his front teeth. Jake was proud of his teeth. Despite his going through twenty cigarettes a day they were snow-white and matinee idol perfect, and he wanted to keep them that way. Harry was no less effeminate today, married, and with a wife who had dropped three kids in less than four years. Thinking about this made him chuckle to himself as Mark got up, having finished his cigarette, to flick the stub out of the window into the yard below. Jake put his out by spitting on it. And now Mark was unbuttoning his shirt…

"Can't hold it in any longer," he drawled, in the gravelly tone that sent shivers down Jake's spine and made his balls flip. "*So* frustrated after that bird let me down last night. A cracker, she was.   The only way I'm going to get her out of my system is to have a J Arthur, and it looks to me that you could do with the same."

"J Arthur?" Jake quizzed him, though he knew very well what he meant.

"J Arthur Rank," Mark retorted. "A ham-shank. Beating the bishop. Fisting the pud…"

Jake shrugged his shoulders as if he was used to seeing this sort of thing every day.

"Why do you need to unbutton your shirt?" he asked.

Mark told him, "It's clean on this morning and I don't want to get it all spunked up. Come on, get your knob out. You'll feel much better afterwards."

Jake hesitated. At school some of the lads in the Sixth Form had held regular wankathons in the changing room, after rugby practice if the games master had not been around. Jake had never participated, but wished that he had because it would have made what he was about to do that much easier. He tried desperately not to let Mark see how thrilled he was to be in close proximity to that magnificent hairy chest—even more so now that their shoulders were touching. Glancing out of his eye corner he swallowed hard as Mark popped the top button of his denims, drew down his zip, took out his cock and began stroking—working the foreskin back over the purple, arrow-shaped helmet. It was not as big as his own cock by a long shot, but Jake decided that it was nice to look at.

Keeping on the grubby T-shirt he had worn yesterday in the turnip field, Jake unzipped his denims, and took out his cock. It was not yet fully hard, but getting there.

"Fucking hell," Mark exclaimed. "There's no wonder you have all the women buzzing around you like flies with a chopper like *that*!"

Jake had by now lost all his inhibitions. He still did not want to risk touching Mark, but was no longer afraid of at least half-watching him as he began beating his meat, the head drooling a clear liquid on to his hairy middle. He only wished that the entertainment might have lasted longer, but such was Mark's excitement than within minutes his rugged features contorted and he let rip, his load bypassing his solar plexus and spattering between his furry pecs, all too much for Jake. Last night he had fantasised about this man and had taken his time. Now he was next to him, panting after his orgasm. Increasing his speed and his grip around his thick shaft, he closed his eyes and banged his big fist against his pelvic bone, the pad of his thumb chafing the underside of his swollen strawberry glans.

"Oh, shit," he groaned, and his balls started to churn and his strawberry helmet flared like an angry cobra.

His first spurter splashed the hem of his T-shirt, but the second was a monster of a ribbon which looped across his body at a forty-five degree angle, finding its target among the streaks on Mark's cum-streaked chest. And there were four more, criss-crossing his T-shirt before his cock stopped pumping and he released it to flop back against the flimsy wet material.

"Bloody hell, Jake," Mark gasped. "You must have been saving that lot up for a month!"

Jake smiled, then he suddenly felt embarrassed.

"I've never done that before," he mumbled, as the colour flooded his lightly-stubbled cheeks.

"Judging by the volume of your load, I'd believe that," Mark chortled.

"I meant that I've never tossed off in front of somebody else," Jake corrected, shoving his semi-hard cock back into his denims and zipping up with some difficulty. "Judging by the mess you've made, you've not done bad yourself."

Mark grinned, and decided not to enlighten Jake that the massive expulsion that he was massaging into his torso was not his own.

"I suppose we'd better get some work done," he said, fastening his shirt. "Your old fella's going to be back before we know it, and we still haven't mucked out the pigs and fed the horses."

Jake descended the rickety ladder first—and backed into Eddie Nelson's arms.

"The old fella's been back some time," Eddie growled. "What have you two been doing up there? I swear to God, Mark Noble, if I smell ale on your breath you'll be heading straight for the bloody dole queue."

Then Eddie saw Mark's half-open shirt and the streaks on his chest…the wet patches down Jake's T-shirt.

"You filthy young bleeder," he yelled, reaching up and fetching Jake one about the ear. "Get back to the house, now. As for you, Mark Noble, I'll deal with you later for perverting my boy."

*

16

It was after eleven when Eddie got back from the Cock & Crown, stinking of beer and in a foul mood. Jake was on his way up to bed when Eddie collared him at the foot of the stairs, and grabbed him by the arm.

"No you don't, laddie," he slurred. "You've got a lot of explaining to do. How long have you been a queer?"

Jake put up a lame argument, "I'm nothing of the kind. We were just mucking around. We were—"

Whack—and Jake was seeing stars as Eddie gave him a crack across the head, not as powerful as the one he had fetched him in the Storm House, but a stinger none the less.

"You're going nowhere until you've explained. I'm not having that kind of behaviour under *my* roof."

"And I've told you," Jake shot back. "We were mucking around, that's all."

Eddie belched loudly, right in Jake's face and almost making him retch. He went for him again, only this time Jake was ready for him. He ducked and, bunching his fist, smacked Eddie under the jaw. For a few seconds, Eddie tottered, his eyes crossing over the bridge of his nose. Then he toppled backwards, banging his head against the wall.

"Get up," Jake snarled at him. "I've had enough of you throwing your weight around. Get up and fight like a man!"

Eddie did not get up. He was out cold. Jake knelt beside him and checked his pulse to see if he was breathing. He was, and he rolled him on to his side just in case he decided to throw up, then raced up the stairs to his room. The next few minutes saw him in a blind panic.

"You could lodge with me," Mark had said.

Grabbing the big suitcase from the top of the wardrobe, Jake threw into it all the things he imagined he would need, at that moment intent on never setting foot inside this house again. His hacking jacket was hanging behind the door. He put this on and clomped back down the stairs. Eddie was still out cold, his wallet half-sticking out of his back pocket. Jake thought for a moment, then grabbed this.

"A small price to pay for all the shit you forced me and Mother to put up with all those years, you evil sod," he spat, before heading for the door.

Then he remembered that tomorrow was Friday, and payday—that Eddie would have been to the bank to draw out the men's wages, and as per usual put the money in the Cadbury's Chocolate Fingers tin in the bottom drawer of the dressing-table, along with his savings. Jake figured the men would be angry, but he was so upset that he no longer cared. He emptied the tin, quickly counted it and realised that there was around three-hundred pounds, much more than he had expected, rolled the banknotes into a bundle, and shoved this into his jacket pocket along with Eddie's wallet.

2: Mark

June 1964

Ten minutes later, Jake was hammering on Mark's door, having sprinted all the way down the hill to Mill Cottage without so much as pausing for breath. And when Mark did not answer straight away, he kept on hammering until the door was flung open.

"Bloody hell, Jake," Mark cried. "Where's the fire?"

He had just stepped out of the tub and was wearing a plaid dressing-gown. Jake shouldered past him and into the living-room. It was the first time he had ever been here.

"I swear to God, I thought for one minute I'd killed the drunken pig," he got out, sinking into one of the two easy chairs in the room and helping himself to a Woodbine from the packet on the arm. "I really did think I'd done him in, and I really wouldn't have cared if I had."

Mark knelt beside him—it seemed the appropriate thing to do, like he was comforting a child.

"Your old man?" he posed. "What's he done this time?"

Jake explained what had happened, all the while riveting his gaze on Mark's half-open dressing-gown, and the hairy chest that had started all of this. He said nothing about the money he had filched.

"Imagine his reaction if he'd turned up earlier and you'd have shot your bolt in his direction and knocked him off that ladder," Mark mused.

"And that isn't even remotely funny," Jake counteracted,

nervously running the fingers of one hand through his hair. "You told me once I could stay here if ever I was in a fix."

Mark stood up. Under the dressing-gown he was getting hard, and rather than face Jake, he walked across to the window and stood with his back to him, gazing outside.

"That might not be a good idea," he said. "Not now…"

"What do you mean, not now?" Jake pressed. "What's happened since you said it'd be okay for me to come here? Were you just kidding me?"

"I wasn't kidding you," Mark replied. "A lot's happened since I said that. This morning, for one thing."

"This morning?" Jake repeated. "Has the old bastard had a go at you as well?"

"He hasn't said a dickie-bird," Mark returned.

"Then what is it?" Jake pressed. "I've packed my bags and I've no intention of *ever* going back there. I thought you'd at least put me up until I've decided what to do next. What have I done wrong, Mark?"

"That's just it, Jake," Mark sighed. "You haven't done *anything* wrong. God, you're not going to like it if I tell you the truth. Then I'll be done for in these parts…"

Jake had every intention of staying. He got up, removed his jacket, and draped it over the back of the chair. Then he sat down again and helped himself to another cigarette from Mark's packet.

"I'm going to like it a lot less if you *don't* tell me what's narking you," he levelled. "I'm not going anywhere till—"

Mark took a deep breath, and turned around to face him.

"I fancy you, Jake. I don't know *when* it happened, and I

don't know *why* it happened. It just did. One minute we were mates, and then…"

"Then you wanted to kiss me," Jake finished. "I've been wanting to kiss *you* for ages. Then I hear people talking about queers and nancy-boys, and keep telling myself that I'm not that way. I only get like it when I'm near you. I like women. I've *always* liked them. What's wrong with me?"

Mark knelt beside him once more. Though his hard-on had subsided, his heart was beating to wildly he expected it to burst any time now.

"There's nothing *wrong* with you, Jake," he said. "It *is* possible to like both—and to find out later in life that you like both, though I've only ever been one way inclined. Do you want to kiss me right now?"

Without waiting for a reply, he stood up and pulled Jake to his feet. The kiss was fumbled, but sufficient to convince him that Jake was probably ready to take things to the next level. He gazed into the large, liquid blue eyes.

"I think we should go upstairs," he said. "We don't have to do any more than we did this morning. Not even that, if you don't want to."

Jake followed him up the narrow staircase. The bedroom ceiling was so low that he could almost touch it with the top of his head. Mark switched on the lamp next to the bed and was initially hesitant to undress. In the eighteen months that he had known Jake, he had never seen him with his top off, even on the hottest day, and had often wondered if this was because he was afraid of him seeing what he may have been hiding underneath—scars, perhaps, inflicted by Eddie.

He had always suspected that he may have been physically violent towards his son, but today was the first time he had seen him hit him. Now, he was relieved that he had been able to express his feelings to an otherwise flagrantly heterosexual young man without Jake smacking him one— for those massive fists looked capable of inflicting some damage, as Eddie had apparently discovered to his chagrin tonight, after finally pushing Jake too far.

"You *are* okay with this?" he asked, as Jake gazed about him, as if looking for hidden cameras or maybe suspecting that someone might have been hiding under the bed or in the wardrobe.

Jake sat on the edge of the mattress, and casting aside all his inhibitions drew his T-shirt over his head. Mark gasped in amazement. There was not a blemish on him, not even the slightest imperfection. Jake was muscular—and how!— with perfectly smooth, deep-cleavaged and lightly tanned pecs which suggested he must have had his kit off at some time, melon biceps, dense jet-black pits, and a delicate love-trail dividing his washboard abs. Mark's cock stiffened at once under his dressing-gown. Then Jake shrugged out of his denims and underpants, and lay on the bed. His cock was not even hard, but even in its flaccid state it was bigger than most that Mark had seen erect.

"So, what now, Mark?" Jake posed. "You're the expert, aren't you?"

Mark was astonished by his composure, the fact that the village stud was lying starkers on *his* bed, albeit not yet in a state of arousal, and treating this new venture so *lightly*.

22

He removed his dressing-gown but, as had happened in the living-room, rather than face Jake walked across to the window and stood there with his back to the bed.

"You've got a hairy arse," Jake observed. "Not that I'm an expert in men's arses. Why don't you turn around?"

"Because I suddenly feel embarrassed," Mark confessed. "We shouldn't be doing this, Jake. *I* shouldn't be doing this. You're not the same as me."

He turned around all the same, bringing a sharp intake of breath from the man on the bed. Jake was not entranced by the rock-hard seven-incher jutting at a forty-five degree angle and hoisting up a more than ample scrotum—he was not particularly thrilled by the muscular thighs and arms, the right one tattooed with a rose. It was that magnificent hairy chest that caused his cock to stir, though only slightly. Mark got on the bed and lay on the bed beside him but not touching him, his hard-on throbbing and drooling a snail's trail across his middle.

"So, what happens now?" Jake asked.

Mark placed one hand on Jake's stomach, and when he flinched and Mark tried to move it away, he found his wrist caught in a grip of steel.

"This is all new to me," he said, gazing into Mark's big brown eyes which looked like they were about to burst into tears. "You'll have to show me what to do…"

Mark could not believe what he was hearing, and a part of him was still thinking that this could all go disastrously wrong at any moment. Yet he had gone this far, and as Jake let go of his wrist he shuddered as his hand moved upwards to cup one pec and then the other, gently tweaking Jake's nipples into fleshy peaks. No one had toyed with his nipples before, and Jake found the sensation surprisingly pleasant, his little sigh of appreciation encouraging Mark to proceed to the next level. Very slowly, he slid his hand downwards over the silky-smooth, warm flesh—over the washboard abs and stopping when he reached the black forest surrounding Jake's still only semi-erect cock. He thought of asking Jake how he was doing, but when he glanced up his eyes were closed and he was smiling like the cat that had found the tub of cream—imagining, Mark assumed, that it was a woman doing this to him and not a rough-and-ready homosexual farmhand.

"That feels nice," Jake murmured. "*Very* nice…"

Mark rolled on to his side and his cock brushed against Jake's lightly-bristled thigh, leaving a little wet patch. Jake reacted by shuffling a little further down the bed and outstretching an arm behind Mark's neck, allowing him to nuzzle the damp, dark tendrils. Few things turned Mark on more than hairy armpits. But his erection was starting to cause him a problem. He needed to reach down and wank out his load before it exploded all over Jake—the way Jake had unknowingly exploded all over him this morning—but he resisted the temptation and instead wrapped his fingers around Jake's cock, worked back his foreskin, and gently masturbated him until he was fully erect.

"Magnificent," he enthused, giving it a squeeze.

Inasmuch as a moment ago he wanted to finish himself off, confident that he would soon be hard again, what Mark *really* wanted was suck this rope-veined monolith, to take the big strawberry-shaped helmet with its grinning slit to the back of his throat. But he wanted something else more. Reluctantly releasing his newfound treasure, he reached across to the drawer in the bedside cabinet for the tub of Vaseline. Jake's contented smile faded.

"Will it hurt a lot?" he asked, in a little boy's voice.

"Probably," Mark told him. "But I'm more than willing to give it a go…"

Jake rolled on to his front, the position he assumed he should have been adopting, and Mark rewarded him with a playful slap across the rump. Jake's arse was no less perfect than the rest of him, the cheeks nice and firm—the crack, when he spread these, nicely hirsute, the mauve virgin bud inviting. But *fucking* Jake was not what he had in mind.

"I want you to make love to me, Jake," he whispered. "The same as you would a woman."

Jake rolled on to his back. The big blue eyes opened very wide.

"You're asking me to shove my knob up your arse?"

Mark groaned, "Well, I would have put it a little more romantically…but yes, I do."

He dipped into the tub of Vaseline, reached under his perineum and lubricated his hole. Then, while Jake was still staring, open-mouthed, he raised his knees to his chin.

"You don't have to look," Mark told him. "I'll guide you. Just pretend you're shoving it inside a fanny. There's not much difference once you get used to it."

Hesitating somewhat, as if afraid of squashing him, Jake

eased his bulk between the wide-spread thighs as Mark hooked his ankles on either side of his neck, in such a way that Jake wouldn't be *able* to look, even if he wanted to. Mark guided the huge weapon until the head was pressed against his sticky ring-muscle.

"Kiss me again," he breathed. "Then just push. But don't push too hard. You *are* rather a big lad…"

The kiss was no less clumsy than before. Five o'clock shadow took some getting used to! Jake pushed, but Mark's sphincter was stubborn and refused to give. Mark realised that he might have been better starting off with a lubricated digit—if nothing else, that Jake would end up coming before her got his cock inside him. Then he figured he was doing well in getting this heterosexual stud to *want* to shove it up there in the first place, without expecting too much of him for his first time. Clapping a hand on each big cheek, and bringing his legs down and clenching them around the small of Jake's back, he forced Jake to penetrate him almost to the hilt in a single thrust.

"Fuck," Mark exclaimed. "It's got corners!"

But if Mark was thinking—or hoping, given the size of the dork deep-rooted inside him and feeling like it might be about to split him in two—that Jake might not last long, he was in for a surprise.

"Wow, it fits," Jake got out. "It feels *so* good…just like the real thing, all nice and tight and lovely and warm!"

Leaning forwards, he kissed Mark again—this time the way he kissed his women, passionately. For fifteen minutes he *fucked* the same way, too—a few short thrusts, followed

26

by a powerful half-dozen fully-penetrating stabs which played havoc with Mark's prostate, causing him to drool on to his belly like a leaky tap. Grabbing his cock, he began stroking furiously, unsure how long Jake would be able to keep going, and hoping they might shoot together. This was impossible when Jake started slamming into him like there was no tomorrow, his features distorted and his torso drenched with sweat. Arching his back and lifting them both up off the mattress, Mark let fly, his first spurter smacking Jake under the chin. Seconds later, Jake exploded like a cannon, his load searing Mark's innards like a white-hot spit. For a few seconds after climaxing he lay motionless on top of him, giving Mark a notion that there might have been more to come. Then he rolled off him and on to his back, his chest heaving like a canoe on a storm-tossed sea.

"Bloody hell, that was summat else," he panted. "I've just had my knob up another man's shitter. I've just fetched inside a bloke's arse…and it was amazing!"

"Erm, I *did* happen to be there," Mark chuckled, his ears still buzzing.

"But it *was* amazing," Jake exclaimed. "How did I do?"

Mark told him, "You did well enough to make me come a bucketload. Well enough to make me think I've died and gone to heaven. Are you *sure* it was your first time with a bloke, Jake?"

"On my own life," Jake retorted. "Why would I want to shove up a man's arse when there's always been a woman around? Well. Until now…"

He paused, initially thinking that it was his heart still pounding like a drum—until he realised that somebody was banging on the door downstairs. Mark jumped off the bed and rushed to the window.

"It's your old man," he said. "He's outside on the path. You'd better stay here while I get rid of him."

Pulling on his denims and the first thing at hand to cover his upper half—Jake's T-shirt—he hurried down the stairs. Leaning against the wall, next to the double-barrel shotgun he used for shooting rabbits, was a crowbar he had left here after doing some work in the back yard. He grabbed this, just in case, and unlatched the door. Eddie, wearing a duffel coat that had seen better days, had been about to barge into the cottage. Seeing the crowbar, he took a step back.

"Where is he?" he growled. "I know he's here. He was seen running down the hill. Somebody told me."

Mark smiled, seeing the bruised and bloodied state that Eddie's face was in after being introduced to Jake's fist, and not a moment too soon. His manner was controlled, though in truth he was terrified, well aware that he had just had sex with a man who, though built like a barn and hung like a bull—not to mention the fact that he had just fucked like one—*was* still legally classed as a minor.

"I don't care what you've been told, Eddie," he levelled. "He's not here. And what have you done to your face? Got pissed again and tumbled over the stile?"

Eddie refused to leave. Jake, standing naked behind the bedroom door and hearing every word, trembled at the very thought of his father storming upstairs.

"That's his T-shirt you're wearing," he spat. "If it isn't, he's got one like it."

"So, we share the same taste in clothes," Mark chortled. "Big deal…"

"Big deal my arse," Eddie now roared. "If he's not here, Mark Noble, you bloody well know where he's gone. He keeps too much company with you. You're a bad influence, you and your queer ways. I don't my son associating with a perverted animal like you."

Mark weighed the curved end of the crowbar against the flat of his hand.

"Would you care to repeat that, Eddie?" he posed. "You're on *my* property. I think you'd better leave—unless you want this shoving where the sun don't shine."

Eddie was adamant and barked, "I'll go when I'm good and ready—when you've told me where he is. Jake's only a kid and he needs to be with his dad."

"The way Pete and Paul needed to be with their dad, you mean?" Mark asked. "They were so eager to get away from you, they moved to the other side of the world. Now fuck off, or I'll blow your brains out."

Dropping the crowbar, he grabbed the shotgun and the cottage seemed to shake on its foundations as it went off. Assuming that Mark had carried out his threat, Jake came rushing down the stairs, his huge cock swinging from side to side, his chest and abs still streaked with Mark's jism. By now Eddie was clobbering up the path in his hobnail boots, but he managed a swansong—turning around seconds after Jake had ducked out of sight.

"Oh, and I forgot to tell you, you queer cunt—you're sacked."

Mark slammed the door shut and drew the bolts. Jake had gone into the living-room and was sitting in the chair he had vacated one hour earlier to embark on the most exciting sexual adventure of his life so far. He was still naked and his legs were spread wide, his cock and balls resting heavily on the embroidered cushion.

"I didn't want to get you into bother," he told Mark. "I certainly didn't want to get you the sack. Maybe I should try talking to him—"

"No bloody way," Mark shot back, grabbing a cigarette and tossing the packet to Jake. "You said you never wanted to go back to that place as long as you lived. That goes for me, even if he changes his mind about sacking me. How do you think I'm going to feel, working for him with this hanging over me?"

"So you're ashamed," Jake began. "You're—"

"Why should I be *ashamed*?" Mark rapped. "I've got the most beautiful man in England sitting bollock-naked in front of me, he's got my spunk all over him, and he's just given me the fuck of a lifetime. If I'm ashamed of anything, it's working for that bigoted twat in the first place. Then again, I would never have met you. Come on, let's go back to bed."

Jake followed him upstairs. Mark undressed and they got into bed. Though it was warm, Mark huddled up to his new lover and lay with his head on his chest, pungent with the aroma of his own recently shot load.

"So, why *did* you come up here to Brodsworthy?" Jake asked him. "You don't have to tell me if you don't want to, but I've always been curious."

The only person until now who had known the real Mark Noble story had been his sister, Mary, now residing in a Doncaster churchyard.

"I've nothing to hide, even though folk around here think I have," he explained. "I was working as a chauffeur down in London, and I got into a spot of bother. My sister married a Yorkshireman and moved to Doncaster. She'd just been widowed and she invited me to come up and stay with her. She died, and I bought this place. That's about it."

Jake suspected that there was more to tell, but he was not interested in pressing. He, the archetypal womaniser, had just kissed and had penetrative sex with another man, and he realised that subconsciously he must have been wanting to get physical with this particular man for some time. If not, why had he found the procedure so utterly normal and intensely pleasurable? What was more, this was no one-off youthful experimentation, for his body was dictating so soon that he wanted to have sex with Mark again. Reaching under the sheets, he wrapped his fingers around Mark's cock, the first time he had touched him intimately since coming here.

*

The next morning, Saturday, Jake awoke feeling better than he had in years. Though he had had done the business with

31

a good twenty women, he had never spent the night with any of them. It had always been *al fresco* sex, or in their homes when their husbands or boyfriends were at work. This was the first time he had woken up in someone else's room, in a bed that was not his own. He got off the bed and stretched, and padded across to the window. It was sunny outside. Birds were twittering in the trees which surrounded the cottage. And he had a rampant hard-on! Then he heard whistling coming from downstairs, and smelled bacon frying. A moment later, Mark breezed into the room. He was wearing his plaid dressing-gown and observed the large slab of man-meat which Jake had rested on the window-sill.

"That looks *very* tasty," he mused. "But first of all you must eat to keep up your strength. Why don't you go have a shower while you're waiting?"

He headed back downstairs, and Jake crossed the landing to the bathroom. The shower that Mark had rigged up over the bath was crude—a hosepipe attached to the taps, with a watering-can rose shoved on to the end. There was no hot water and Jake shivered as he quickly soaped himself clean. Then, wrapping a towel about his middle and using another to dry himself, he returned to the bedroom. Two minutes later, Mark arrived with a tray containing bacon sandwiches and a pot of tea.

"So, what happens next?" Jake asked, tossing the towels aside and flopping on to the bed. "Obviously I can't stay here, not with the old man on the warpath."

"Nor can I," Mark told him. "Your father's got a mouth

the size of a gas oven. By now the whole village is going to know about how I've perverted Eddie Nelson's son. Never mind that it takes two to tango. First thing Monday morning I'll have to down the Labour Exchange and sign on. And seeing as I've been sacked, I won't get any benefits for six weeks. Those are the rules, Jake. Good job I've got a little put aside for a rainy day, for the way I see it, it's going to be pissing down for a long time."

3: An Enforced Parting

June 1964

Monday came too quickly. They had spent three nights and days together, like lovebirds. Three nights in succession, they had made love, with Jake always on top, always with absolutely no foreplay, always in the same position. Mark accepted that this was new territory for the young man, and hoped that in time he would teach him to be a little more adventurous and convince him that there was much more to man-and-man love-making than straight-to-it penetration, even though Jake *was* inordinately good at this.

After lunch, and after making Jake promise to keep the door locked and open it for no one until he returned, Mark drove the five miles into Doncaster. His first port of call was the Labour Exchange, where a clerk told him he would have to come back tomorrow to sign on.

Last night, he and Jake had talked about their future. By coincidence their favourite seaside resort was Whitby, the little fishing town on the east coast of Yorkshire. Mark had been there often since coming up from London and enjoyed its easy-going tranquility. As a child Jake had been taken here many times by his aunt, now deceased. Mark had told Jake of his plans. He would put the cottage up for sale so that they could relocate to Whitby—work-wise, they would cross that bridge when they came to it. Mark did not care what people might have been saying about *him*, but he was worried about what they might have been saying about Jake and assumed that once word got out about his latent homosexuality—though there was no proof of this, other than Eddie catching the aftermath of the wank in the Storm House—the boy's name would be mud.

Mark's fears were confirmed when he parked his car in the garage he rented behind the Cock & Crown, a necessity because the lane leading to the cottage was too narrow and steep to drive down. Bob, the landlord, was out watering his window-boxes and shouted to him as he was crossing the road towards the top of the lane.

"Morning, Mark," he pronounced. "We've not seen Jake around in here for a while. The last I heard, he had a bit of trouble sitting down."

Mark ignored him, and carried on walking. It was just before six when he reached the cottage. Jake unbolted the door, and told him there had been no unwelcome visitors— just the postman with the electricity bill. After dinner they watched the television until eleven, not really taking much notice of what was happening on the screen. While Jake was doing the washing up, Mark went upstairs and had a shower—Jake's hair was damp, suggesting he had done so already. When Mark returned to the living-room, a towel wrapped about his waist, his rugged face wore a hard-set expression. Each in his chair in front of the empty grate, they smoked in silence—Mark feeling glum because their idyll here was coming to an end, certainly for now…Jake feeling edgy because there *had* been an unwelcome visitor.

While he had been peeling the potatoes earlier, the letterbox had rattled, and a man's voice had yelled through

35

the aperture, "Fucking queers!"

In the bedroom, Mark cheered up somewhat and told Jake, "For the past three nights, *you've* been the one doing all the work. Why don't you lie on your stomach? I have a nice little surprise for you."

Jake did as requested, stretching out with his long legs slightly apart and telling himself that this had always been bound to happen—that Mark would end up wanting to fuck him, and that when the time came he would have to grin and bear it. Mark lost the towel. His cock was upstanding, and lying on top of Jake he wedged it between his warm, firm buttocks and began nuzzling the back of his neck.

"You're going to shove it inside me," Jake murmured. "It's probably going to hurt like hell, but it's only fair that I give it a go…"

Mark worked his way down Jake's spine, executing little butterfly kisses which made him shudder but which felt so inordinately good.

"I'm going to do nothing you don't want me to do," he breathed. "Any time you want me to stop, I will. I promise."

With his teeth Mark tugged at the fine hairs above Jake's tailbone, before using the flats of his hands to part the firm, bulbous globes. Jake was astonishingly hirsute here, a thick sooty haven lining the deep trench all the way along his perineum and all but concealing his small, tight-puckered virgin bud. Such was the sensation when Mark poked the point of his tongue inside this exquisitely-flavoured orifice that Jake wanted to scream out loud. The most any of his female conquests had ever done had been to briefly suck his cock, and on his part there had rarely been much in the way of preliminaries. It had usually been a case of getting hard, and slamming home. But this—this was a whole new world of ecstasy!

Jake's response to was to instinctively raise his rump off the mattress, and Mark devoured his sphincter for a little while longer until assured that it was time to move to the next level. Grabbing the Vaseline, he smeared a liberal amount of the sticky gunge around Jake's back entrance, parting his anal forest like the Red Sea, and poked the tip of his index finger inside.

"Are you *sure* you haven't done this before?" he asked, surprised at how relaxed Jake's ring-muscle had become with so little teasing.

"On my life," he got out. "God, that doesn't half feel nice…"

Mark very gently pushed his forefinger inside him up to the second knuckle, locating his prostate at once. Satisfied that Jake felt comfortable with his, he frigged him gently.

"How does that feel?" he asked.

"Like I want to fetch," Jake panted. "Like when I had my first wank and wondered what the hell was happening."

Mark thought it prudent to remove his digit—he did not want to make Jake "fetch" just yet! Coaxing him on to his knees, he positioned his helmet against the well-greased hole. Last night—indeed, as with every time they hit the sheets—Jake had slammed into *him* like a crashing train, something Mark put down to youthful inexperience. Taking it from Jake *had* hurt, but only for a moment until he had become accustomed to the lad's length and inordinate girth. Now, Mark inserted just the arrow-shaped head of his cock, while winding his arms around Jake's tautened middle, and licking the soft, smooth flesh between his shoulder-blades. Very, *very* slowly he began moving inside him, gradually working his way in until Jake had taken all seven inches. Only then did he let his hands to drop—one to caress Jake's low-hanging, boxer's glove scrotum, the other to stroke his massive rod. Jake had always liked to control the action, but he was now at his lover's mercy and enjoying every second of Mark's domination—but oh, so dangerously edging! He whimpered, like a faun dragged away from suckling its mother, hardly the sound Mark expected to come from a stud with muscles in his spit.

"I can stop if you want me to," Mark breathed. "I mean, if I'm causing you discomfort…"

"Shut up, Mark," came the growled response. "Keep on going till you make us both fetch."

The fuck was a long one. Mark would have preferred to change position in order to observe the expression on Jake's face when he climaxed, but he considered himself fortunate to have got this far with the village lothario, and though his thighs were starting to cramp up he kept thrusting upwards, harder and deeper—until he exploded. Jake groaned as the hot sperm seared his bowels, though by now he had reached the point of no return. Still deep-rooted inside him, Mark tightened his grip on Jake's cock and wanked him with unaccustomed fury until, with a almighty roar, he bucked his hips and cannoned a good half-dozen spurts of jism across the counterpane and the headboard.

*

The next morning after breakfast—it was warm already and they were lounging in front of the cottage with their shirts off, next to the little stream—Mark reiterated their plans for the future, which would necessitate their separating for a while, and the sooner the better. Jake saw no sense in this. Then Mark explained.

"I'm tied to this place, Jake," he said. "I can't just up and leave. Daft as it sounds, what we've done is illegal. You've got the biggest cock I've ever seen and you fuck like a stud bull, but in the eyes of the law you're classed as a child. I could actually go to prison for letting *you* fuck *me*. We shouldn't even be out here. If anybody sees us…"

Jake no longer cared if anybody saw them or not—to the outside world, two friends out in the fresh air, enjoying the morning sunshine, albeit that Mark's hairy chest, glistening with perspiration, was starting to give him one hell of a hard-on. He could also have told Mark that *he* could also be in serious trouble. He had lifted his father's wallet, and Eddie would already have gone to the Chocolate Fingers tin and found the men's wages gone. He was surprised that the police had not come here already, asking questions.

"Fucking *queers*," the man had yelled through the letter-Box, loud enough to be heard in the village—not *queer*, but in the plural.

39

"They must have seen me looking out of the window," Jake thought to himself.

And Mark was asking, "Jake—have you heard of a man called Tommy Vincent?"

Jake pondered for a moment, and shook his head.

"Should I have?"

"I guess not," Mark replied. "Tommy manages pop stars. He's one of the biggest managers in the business. The bees' knees, as they say down in London."

"And what does that have to do with the price of fish?" Jake wanted to know.

Mark explained, "I worked for him—one of his drivers. He's one of us, if you get my drift. We still keep in touch. I was on the blower to him. He's looking for a temporary chauffeur. He owes me a favour, and when I told him I had a friend who was in a bit of a fix, he thinks you might just fit the bill."

He lay back in the grass, with his hands behind his head, exposing his sooty pits. Jake could not resist threading his fingertips through the carpet of bristles on his chest. Mark reciprocated by reaching up and tweaking a nipple. What he really wanted to do was rip off the rest of Jake's clothes and encourage him have him, here next to the rippling stream, but he naturally resisted the urge.

"Let's get this straight," Jake said. "You worked for this bloke in London, and he's looking for another driver and he's interested in somebody who lives—what, two-hundred miles away? Don't they have any drivers down there?"

"Not like you," Mark could not resist saying. "Seriously,

though. Tommy helped me out when I was in a fix. He owes me. I think you should give it a go, until I've sorted out things up here. I mean, what do you have to lose?"

"You, for starters," Jake replied. "Apart from a couple of school trips and the ones to Whitby with my aunt, I've never travelled any further than town. It'll be a whole new world down there, one I mightn't like. I know it's only early days. You've made me feel better than a *dozen* women ever could. I won't care what folks say if you won't. Can't we just stick it out and see what happens?"

Mark sighed. He loved the way Jake was touching him, and he *never* wanted them to be apart, not even for a day.

"Sweetheart," he pleaded. "Do you really think folks are going to believe we're living together only as mates? It's different in London. Nobody cares what anybody does so long as they're not scaring the birds. Go down there—and as soon as I've got shot of this place, we can start afresh somewhere else."

"But this Tommy Vincent," Jake pressed. "Who is he— an old flame of yours?"

Mark shook his head, "I told you, he manages pop stars and he helped me out over a bit of bother. He owes me."

Jake pressed him, but Mark was not saying.

"We all have our little secrets that we like to keep all to ourselves," was all that he would say.

Jake found this amusing. His *big* secret was in his jacket pocket—all three-hundred pounds of it.

*

They spent the evening watching television. They had known each other as friends for eighteen months, during which time Jake confessed to having had sex with nineteen women—twenty, if he counted the wank from Amy Rogers in the post office yard. He had never made fun of homosexuals the way some did, or insulted them, his theory being live and let live. And he had *never* had homosexual thoughts until seeing Mark with his shirt off in the turnip field. He guessed though that these must have been there, lurking under the surface, otherwise he would have rejected Mark's advances and not had sex with him quite so readily and found this perfectly normal.

Now he was leaving all this behind and acknowledged the fact that Mark was right—that he *had* to make himself scarce. It was either that or return to the farm, which would only be slightly more preferable than running naked into a burning building. Mark had told him what the landlord at the Cock & Crown had shouted. By now the whole village would have denounced him as a pervert. He remembered Adele Stevens, who cleaned at the vicarage. When Adele had fallen pregnant a few years ago, the tittle-tattlers had speculated who the father might have been, until someone had posted a photo of Ken Jones on the church noticeboard. Adele had been sent to her aunt's in Durham until after her confinement, and her mother had told everyone that her baby had died so that no one would find out it had been put up for adoption. As for poor Ken, he had done a runner and not been seen since. Jake told himself, if there had been a to-do about these two so-called "normal" people, then what

Mark said about them going through hell, should they stay together at his cottage, would come true. Then he thought about the money he had stolen from his father, hopefully more than enough to get him to London and see him right until Mark had sorted things out up here.

Their lovemaking that night was no less thrilling than before, but tinged with sadness because it was their last for a while. Over breakfast, they even discussed the possibility of Jake staying here—of Mark *not* putting the cottage up for sale and finding work locally, and to hell with Eddie Nelson and the gossips who in any case had no proof of what was taking place once the door was locked and the curtains closed. This changed when Mark went into the living-room and opened the curtains. Daubed in red paint across the window-pane were the words "QUEER BASTARDS".

Twenty minutes later, Jake's suitcase was packed and—as they were about to leave and walk up the lane to where Mark had parked his car—Jake remembered something.

"My watch. I think I left it under my pillow…"

He rushed up the stairs into the bedroom. Taking thirty pounds from his father's wallet—enough to tide Mark over, he figured, should he run short while waiting for his unemployment benefit—he placed this on the cabinet under the tub of Vaseline. A moment later he joined Mark.

"It was on my wrist all the time," he observed, meaning his watch.

It was just after ten when they set off for Doncaster railway station. And as if they were not feeling sufficiently downhearted, Eddie Nelson's Thames Trader passed them on the opposite side of the road a mile from the town. Eddie blared his horn and pulled up as if to turn around and follow them, but if this was his intention, much to Jake's relief he changed his mind.

"Shame about that," Mark gruffed. "I'm in the mood for breaking that fucker's jaw, right now."

The twenty minutes they spent waiting on the crowded platform for the delayed London train were sheer agony for Mark, who wanted to take Jake in his arms and devour him with kisses, regardless of their scenario. Jake only hoped that the train would not turn up, that they would get fed up of hanging around and head back to Mark's cottage, and re-think their dilemma from there.

Then it all happened so very quickly. The train arrived, and there was panic as everyone tried to board at once—the previous train had not turned up and there was a shortage of seats. All they managed was a quick hug, and a peck on the cheek from Mark.

"I love you, Jake Nelson," he murmured.

4: London

July 1964

Less than an hour after Mark had parked his car behind the Cock & Crown—he was in the kitchen preparing lunch, and feeling miserable as sin—there was a hammering on the front door, so loud that the building seemed to shake.

"If that's Eddie Nelson, I swear to God I'm gonna wring his neck," he grumbled, wiping his hands and going to see who this was.

It *was* Eddie, in his shabby work-clothes and smelling of the farmyard. Standing next to him was a young fair-haired constable, Jeff Collins, with whom Mark had a history.

"I want to see my boy," Eddie snarled. "I know he's in there because he's been seen."

"Like he was seen running down the hill the other night, Eddie?" Mark quizzed. "I told you before, he's not here."

"Then you won't mind me taking a squint around the place?" Jeff asked, offering Mark a sly wink from behind Eddie's back.

"Be my guest," Mark said, and as he shouldered past him and entered the cottage, he whispered in Jeff's ear, "I think it's time we had another reunion. Know what I mean?"

Jeff coloured. He had not wanted to come here, but his sergeant had assigned the duty to him, and he had been in no position to argue. Three months ago, he and Mark had enjoyed a very pleasant, sex-filled weekend—in Whitby.

"I'll make a note of it in my diary," he responded.

Jeff checked the kitchen, the living room and upstairs—and the outbuildings, when Eddie persisted. There was no sign of Jake, not that Jeff would have said anything, if there *had* been. He owed it to Mark not to get him into bother, and put the kibosh on their "reunion"!

"Well, he *was* here," Eddie sneered. "Being perverted by this bastard."

"Don't you mean by this *queer* bastard?" Mark pressed, pointing to the graffiti on the window. "I don't suppose *you* would know anything about that, would you?"

"Nowt to do with me," Eddie growled. "I'm not the only one round here with an opinion. The little shit also ran off with my money—pinched my wallet and three-hundred quid out of the tin where I keep my savings and the men's wages . I don't suppose *you* know anything about that?"

Mark shook his head. He genuinely had not known this, but he guessed this explained the thirty pounds that he had found under the tub of Vaseline.

"Three-hundred pounds," he echoed. "Who in their right mind keeps that amount of cash in the house?"

"That's no reason for him to pinch it," Eddie argued. "And if he *hasn't* been here, I'm sure you'll know where he is. You two have always been thick as thieves."

Mark told him, "I didn't say he *hadn't* been here, Eddie. He *was* here, but only long enough to have a bottle of beer and tell me what a pig you are, as if I didn't already know. That's *three* sons you've driven away from home."

Eddie hawked and spat, nodded to Jeff Collins, and then

clomped along the path towards the gate. Jeff waited until he was out of earshot.

"You and Jake Nelson, bumming another," he chortled. "If you ask me, there's as much chance of that one turning the other way as I have of growing an extra head."

"My thoughts exactly," Mark said.

Then Jeff grabbed a handful and continued, "As for the other—I'm on late shifts until Friday, and then I've got the weekend off. Why don't I pick you up at seven?"

Mark nodded, "Yes, I think I'd like that."

*

Jake found his very first long train journey frustrating, to say the least. Because the previous train had missed, he found himself sitting in the aisle until Peterborough, then ended up sitting opposite vicar who kept staring at him.

"It's as if he knows what I've been up to, these last few nights," he thought to himself.

Mark had given him a slip of paper upon which he had scribbled Tommy Vincent's address and directions how to get there, having assured him for the umpteenth time that there was nothing to worry about, that Tommy would be expecting him. Jake was not so naïve to be unaware that there could be more to this than met the eye. He was also suspicious of just about everyone surrounding him as he left King's Cross and walked past the row of black taxis.

"*Take a cab*," Mark had advised him. "*London has some very long streets.*"

When Jake asked one of the drivers how much it would cost to take him to his destination—Argyll Street—he was so shocked by the price he quoted that he opted to walk. He soon discovered that Mark had been right. London *did* have some long streets! His first port of call was a branch of the bank he used back home where he handed the clerk his paying-in-book and the three-hundred pounds he had lifted from his father. The money in Eddie's wallet, he estimated, would tide him over for a while. When he saw the tariffs in the entrances to some of the hotels, he was not so sure.

"Bloody hell," he muttered to himself. "I could live for a week on what they're charging for one night down here!"

Neither was he impressed by the building belonging to the address that Mark had given him—like all the others in the street several storeys high, and looking like the exterior had not seen a lick of paint in decades. A brass plaque on the wall next to the door listed the names of the inhabitants: a doctor, two solicitors, a dentist's surgery, but no Tommy Vincent. Jake walked in and approached the desk with the sign "Concierge", though he had no idea what this meant, and showed the woman sitting behind it the scrap of paper that Mark had given him.

"Top floor," she told him, seemingly without moving her lips. "They don't like to advertise the fact."

There was a lift—a cage contraption which rattled and swayed from side to side, making Jake wish he had taken the stairs. There was just one door on the landing, which bore the sign "THOMAS J VINCENT ENTERPRISES". Jake tapped on this, and a voice yelled for him to enter. He found himself in a small room, pretty much like a doctor's waiting-room, containing just two chairs and a pot-plant. In front of him was a glass-partitioned hatch, and to his right a door marked "PRIVATE". Sitting behind the partition was a middle-aged woman in a tweed top who looked like a character from an Agatha Christie murder-mystery. She was even wearing a hat like the one Jake he had seen Margaret Rutherford wearing in *Murder She Said* at the village cinema two weeks ago. He handed her the slip of paper, and she smiled and handed him a key. He relaxed somewhat, knowing that he had been expected.

"The address is on the tag," she said. "Your digs, around the corner in the next street. We weren't sure you'd turn up. There'll be something better if you meet with Mr. Vincent's approval. He's out for the rest of the day. He'll see you in the morning—ten o'clock sharp, and try not to be late."

Jake's "digs" were housed in a building in an even worse state of repair than the one he had just vacated. Here there was no *concierge*, just a dusty staircase reeking of cat-piss and which spiralled upwards through several levels. His room was on the third floor, and like nothing he had seen before. Partridge Farm may have been miserable when Eddie Nelson had been in a foul mood, which was most of the time, but it had been clean because a woman had come in three times a week to ensure that it stayed spic-and-span as his mother had kept it. This room smelled foisty, the furniture looked like it had been dug out of the corporation tip—and the bed, kinking in the middle, looked like it had a life of its own. Tossing his suitcase on to it, surprised that it did not raise a cloud of dust, Jake went to the sink and washed his face as best he could—there was no soap—and dried it on the threadbare towel.

At seven, he found himself in Chinatown, where for the first time he ate noodles, and Chow Mein that had not come out a Vesta packet—a treat at home instead of the regular, boring meat and two veg, but only when his father was not home. Eddie Nelson hated all foreigners, blacks, Chinese, gypsies, homosexuals, and anything associated with them.

A little after eight, Jake ended up down the road in Soho, which very definitely *was* a whole new world: strip-clubs, revues, theatre hoardings advertising *Half A Sixpence* and *Pickwick*, names on hoardings such as Bob Monkhouse, Harry Secombe and Tommy Steele that he had only seen on the television or in the newspapers…and ticket prices way out of his pocket range, had he been interested in seeing any of these shows. The pubs he found fascinating, but again expensive. He could buy two pints of beer back home for what it cost for one down here—beer that was flat as a fart because it had no top on it, but good beer just the same.

It was Jake's luck that he ended up at the Golden Lion, in Dean Street. The place stank of stale sweat and beeswax, and the décor reminded him of Grandma Nelson's outdated drawing-room: flock wallpaper, faded pictures on the walls, and a smoke-stained ceiling that had not been whitewashed in years. The clientele reminded him of the regulars in the tap-room at the Cavalier Arms—the pub in the next village

50

that his mother had said was always full of mucky old men: shifty-looking characters with lived-in faces, along with one or two middle-aged men who Jake was not quite sure if they *were* men. Only the song coming from the jukebox—Dusty Springfield begging her lover, "Stay Awhile"—made him feel that he did not want to turn around and walk back out of the door.

"What'll it be, duck?" the tubby balding barman chirped as Jake studied the row of beer pumps. "Plenty to choose from, and I'm not just talking about the ale."

Jake coloured, realising at once the sort of establishment he was in, but too late to leave as he nodded towards the pump marked "London Pride", and the man started pulling his drink. He had heard some of the more-travelled villagers talking about London's "queer bars"—how if you wandered into one by mistake to make sure if you dropped your wallet never to bend down unless your back was facing the wall. Eddie Nelson's brother—Uncle Roy, who had served with the Royal Marines and seen more of the world than anyone else in the family, though not the brightest button in the box—once remarked that drinking the beer in one of these establishments was "enough to turn a normal man bent". Jake chuckled to himself recalling this, and wondered what Roy would have to say about his nephew having already "turned". Leaning against the bar, he was sipping his beer—and wondering what Mark was doing right now—when he realised that, so soon, he had company.

"Hello handsome. Haven't seen *you* in here before!"

He was tall, in his late twenties, with piercing light grey eyes, angular cheekbones, almost shoulder-length blond hair and a floppy fringe. He was wearing tight black leather trousers, the crotch of which left little to the imagination, and a white vest which exaggerated his not inconsiderable muscles, and over this a black leather waistcoat.

"Maybe that's because I've not been here before," he gruffed, trying not to sound too taken aback. "I arrived in London this afternoon—still feeling my way around."

The man seemed amused by this, and stuck out his hand. Jake winced as he was caught in a steely grip.

"A Northerner," he pronounced in a Cockney accent not dissimilar to Mark's, though the voice was softer. "So—are you buying, or selling? I'm Ricky, by the way."

"Jake," he responded. "Am I buying or selling what?"

Ricky sniggered at this, though not in an offensive way, "You really don't know, do you? Tell him, Jack."

The barman leaned over the counter. His halitosis made Jake flinch, and his East End patter was incomprehensible.

"You can get anyfink you want here, son," he whispered. "A sailor fresh out of the docks if you have the spondoolies. But if you're flogging it in here, you have to come to me first and it's ten per cent for the management—otherwise you hawk your mutton outside in the street and risk being nabbed by the Old Bill."

Jake did not have a clue what Jack was talking about.

"That was all double-Dutch to me," he said as the man waddled away to serve a customer.

Ricky said, "Not double-Dutch, treacle. It's what comes

with being born within the sound of Bow Bells. Jack's curious as to whether you're renting out, or if you're some rich boy looking for a bit of fun. The accent excludes you from being a Dilly Boy."

"And you're not making much more sense," Jake told him. "Why don't you talk in English so I can understand?"

Ricky indicated a vacant table. They took their drinks there, and he elaborated.

"You really are a stranger in these parts, aren't you?" he posed. "Didn't you know what *kind* of joint this was before you walked in that door, or are you pulling my wick?"

Jake responded, trying not to look into Ricky's eyes, "I was thirsty and wanted a pint. Where I come from, that's what boozers are for, aren't they?"

Ricky pulled a packet of cigarettes out of his waistcoat pocket—du Maurier—and handed one to Jake.

"Jake," he levelled, opting for the more direct approach. "Are you competition? Are you on the game?"

Jake shook his head, "What gave you that impression?"

Ricky sighed loudly. This boy really *was* green around the gills!

"Jake, do you ever look in the mirror and take any notice of what you see? You're absolutely drop-dead gorgeous. Yours is the face that would give a dead man a hard-on. I can well imagine the rest of you ain't that bad, either."

For Jake, the penny had dropped.

"You think I'm a prozzie?" he demanded harshly. "A prozzie that goes with other blokes? Is that what *you* are?"

Ricky nodded, "Yes, but we don't use words like that in

this neck of the woods. The vulgar term is rent-boy, but I prefer to call myself a Dilly Boy. So—what's it to be?"

Jake had finished his drink and replied, "Mine's London Pride, a pint of."

Ricky guffawed at this, and so did Jack, behind the bar.

He said, lowering his voice, "What I mean, Jake, is what can I do for you? I'm feeling rather generous tonight. What do you say to me taking you out the back and giving you a nice, slow hand-job—on the house, of course?"

"I'd tell you to fuck off," Jake barked. "And now I suppose I've offended you?"

Ricky chuckled at this, "Dear heart, in my line of work insults bounce off like water off a duck's back. Don't you at least fancy me a *little* bit?"

Jake shook his head, though when Ricky flashed a sexy smile straight out of a toothpaste commercial, he was not so sure. Until now, he had considered Mark a one-off, but there was something about this man that appealed to him.

"Then why have you come in here and started talking to me?" Ricky asked him. "You're not a copper, are you—an *agent-provocateur*?"

"I came in here for a drink," Jake stressed. "It was *you* who came talking to me. No, I'm not a copper, or whatever that other thing is you thought I was. I work on a farm in Yorkshire. Well, I *did*…"

The beer, when he got around to his third pint—stronger than the beer back home—loosened Jake's tongue, and he explained how he had had a barney with his father, of how a friend had put him in touch with someone in London who might offer him a job. He said nothing about stealing the money, or about Mark. And when he mentioned Tommy Vincent's name, Ricky's face lit up.

"The geezer who manages all the pop stars? He comes in here, every now and then. A Jewish boy who started off without two halfpennies to scratch his arse with—reckoned to be worth a fair bob now. Gave me a twenty quid once, to wank *me* off. He's a nice bloke, is Tommy Vincent, but if he's offered you a job, there's bound to be a catch. There always is."

"That's what I told my friend," Jake said. "He's not involved with the underground, is he—the Krays and that sort of stuff?"

Ricky shrugged his shoulders, "Who knows what these rich boys get up to? What I mean is, he'll probably expect you to drop your trousers like he does everybody else. They reckon he's shagged every singer on his books, and that they've all gone a long way in the business because they've *let* him shag them."

"Well, he'll be barking up the wrong tree if that's what he's expecting from me," Jake told him. "I have a girlfriend up in Yorkshire. Several, as it happens…"

Half an hour later, after changing the subject and talking about more regular topics—what kind of women he liked, the shocking difference in prices between London and up North, and the Profumo scandal, Jake shook hands with Ricky and left the pub.

It was a humid night, and rather than risk sleeping on the bed Jake stripped naked, and lay on top of it, hoping that he would not wake up itching in the morning. He thought about Ricky, the way he had jumped to the conclusion that *he* of all people had gone in there with one aim—to sell his body to other men! Jake wondered what Ricky would have had to say, had he told him that until very recently he had never *dreamed* of having sex with another man, and that he was far from experienced in such things—but now that he had dipped his toe into the water, so to speak, he was eager to see how far he could swim.

He reflected on what the loquacious blond had said about Tommy Vincent, and wondered what he might be letting himself in for—some hideous-looking old lecher wanting to shove his cock up his arse. Then his thoughts turned to Mark, that mouth-wateringly hairy chest and how good it had been, making love to him, how surprisingly thrilling when Mark had returned the compliment. It was just another hole, Mark had said, the only difference being was that it was in a different place than Jake was used to. But it had *not* been just another hole, it had been the entrance to paradise!

Thinking about Mark brought about a stirring down below, and the familiar tingling in the pit of his stomach. Reaching down he wrapped his fingers around his cock and began stroking. Closing his eyes, he saw Mark's rugged but handsome face, then Ricky's near-angelic one, the innocent expression belying the fact that he was on the game, and not interested in anyone unless they were dipping into their wallet. And it was this face that he saw as he blasted his load across his middle, and seconds later he fell asleep.

The next morning, Jake awoke early and with a slightly fuzzy head on account of the four pints of London Pride he had quaffed the evening before. There were no washing facilities in the tawdry room other than the sink, but there was a shower-room on the landing. There was no lock on the door and the fibreglass curtain was ripped, enabling anyone who walked in to catch an eyeful. He showered hurriedly—the water was lukewarm and he was unable to shave—and wrapping the towel about him returned to his room and dressed, putting on black slacks and a white, short-sleeve shirt. It was too warm to wear a jacket, and his only suit—a black one bought for his mother's funeral—was back at Partridge Farm. He figured that if Tommy Vincent did not like him as he was, he would have to find somebody else for his thus far suspicious job.

The same woman was sitting behind the glass partition, wearing the same hat as yesterday but not the same tweed top. This time she smiled warmly, and got up to unlatch the door marked PRIVATE.

"You're early," she said, nodding to the door at the far end of the room which Jake assumed was Tommy Vincent's office. "Mr. Vincent will like that. Take a seat and I'll fetch you some coffee. Or would you prefer tea?"

Jake told her that coffee would do fine, though he had rarely touched the stuff at home. While waiting he tried to imagine what Tommy Vincent would look like. Ricky had said he was Jewish, so he guessed he might either look like Frankie Vaughan, his mother's favourite crooner—or like Fagin in the Alec Guinness film. This latter caused him to

57

shudder—the thought of someone like that sniffing around all those good-looking pop singers, and worse still sniffing around him. Then the office door opened, and Jake caught his breath much as he had that first time he had seen Mark shirtless in the turnip field.

Tommy Vincent was in his mid-thirties and was not of course bare-chested, but the white shirt he was wearing was split almost to the waist on account of the heat, revealing a pleasant expanse of neatly-trimmed black bristles. He was not a tall man—five-eight, if that. Neither did he ressemble Fagin, and he was ten times better looking than Frankie Vaughan. He held out his hand, and the touch was electric.

"So, how *is* my old mucker, Mark Noble?" he asked, the Etonesque voice only very slightly effete, showing Jake into an office which looked like it had come out of a *Hollywood Homes* commercial.

"Mark's good," Jake told him. "Well, he's out of a job at the moment, but he's okay."

"Mark's a survivor," Tommy grinned, displaying slightly crooked but perfectly white teeth. "What he's been through, he would have to be. But enough of that for now. How are you finding London so far?"

He indicated one of half-a-dozen leather-covered easy chairs strategically place in front of his leather-topped desk.

"Expensive," Jake replied, sinking into his seat. "Very expensive, compared to what I'm used to."

Glancing about him, he recognised some of the faces in the framed pictures on the walls: Adam Faith, Billy Fury, Lennie Stevens, Tony Milano, Eddie Westbrook—not one woman amongst the gallery of household names, and Jake recalled what Ricky had said, about Tommy Vincent having bedded them all.

"I call them my kids," Tommy smiled. "Well, most of them. A few I book just now and then for the odd gig or tour. Lennie Stevens is my biggest star, and he knows it, by God. I think you two will get along fine, if you decide to take the job."

Jake's eyes opened wide at this.

The previous year, Lennie Stevens had topped the charts with "I'm Not The Man You Think I Am". One of Jake's girlfriends had put it on the turntable while they had been having sex—he had been lying on the shag-pile carpet with her riding him, and had been in the throes of shooting his load when she had climbed off him to put on the flip-side, ruining the whole experience.

"His *chauffeur*, providing your credentials are in order," Tommy corrected, with a little laugh. "And now that I've seen how powerfully built you are I guess you could double as his minder, which will be reflected in the salary. Tell me, Jake. How much did you earn as a farm labourer?"

Jake showed him his driver's licence, clean as a whistle, though he was not sure if Tommy meant this when he said credentials, or something else—and told him, his father had paid him a fiver a week.

"That's not bad, in today's economy," Tommy said. "What would you say if I offered you *four* fivers a week, plus free and gratis lodgings far better than the shit-hole my secretary booked you into for last night? Take your time…"

"Twenty quid," Jake muttered. "There's got to be a catch somewhere..."

"There's *always* a catch, dear boy," Tommy responded, indicating to the pictures on the walls. "I'll level with you, Jake. I have twenty-two artists on my books. They all look like movie stars, and I've had every one of them with the exception of Lennie Stevens. Out of those twenty-two, Mr. Stevens notwithstanding I can put my hand on my heart and confidently say that less than half of them would be able to hold a note in key if they tried."

"I've got records by some of them, and they sound good enough to me," Jake counteracted.

"It's the recording studio that *makes* them sound good," Tommy argued. "That and the fact that when they're on the stage the girls are too busy screaming to realise they're tone deaf—or bent as nine-bob notes. Why not have a cigarette, Jake, while you're mulling things over?"

Jake reached across to the box on Tommy's desk—du Maurier, the same brand as Ricky had smoked last night. He decided that he would smoke this, but he had already "mulled things over".

"Okay," Tommy levelled. "I'll pay you *thirty* pounds a week. You'd have to work every hour of the day, seven days a week to earn that on your Yorkshire farm. And..."

"*And* what?" Jake posed.

"And I get to fuck you over the end of my desk, like I have all the others," Tommy finished, bold as brass.

Jake had expected something like this after what Ricky had said, though not for the impresario to be *so* direct. He also realised that *he* was holding the aces. Stubbing out his cigarette, he got up out of the chair and Tommy caught his breath. These boys *never* turned him down. In the past he had always offered them enough money not to, and with the promise of more to come! And now this farm boy—this gorgeous hunk from up North who didn't even know how to pronounce his aitches—was doing just this! His heart started pounding. What if Jake ran squealing to the police? Tommy had seen his date-of-birth on his driver's license.

"Excuse me, officer. I've been for an interview and this bloke offered me the job at six times the going rate—so long as he can bum me over the end of his desk!"

Then he relaxed, as Jake stuck out his hand.

"It's a deal," he said, and then added, looking Tommy in the eye, "But *I'll* be the one doing the fucking, and it won't be over the end of a desk—and it won't be here."

"Fair enough," Tom smirked. "I'll look forward to that."

*

Tommy Vincent had given Jake an address in Mayfair, and told him to take the Tube to Green Park, and then hail a cab. It was the first time he had been on an underground train and he found the experience scary, but exhilarating. Coming out of the station, however, he decided that he needed some Dutch courage and stopped off at a pub where he ordered a double whisky and smoked two cigarettes while pondering over the evening ahead.

Not so long ago Maisie Clarke, the landlady of the Cock

& Crown—had shouted to him from her bedroom window that if he and Susan Edwards didn't stop making so much noise while fucking up against the wall in the pub's back yard, she would come downstairs and empty a bucket of water on them. Jake wondered what Maisie's reaction would have been had this been two men—doubtless he would be enjoying Her Majesty's pleasure right now. Mark had since taught him the joys of man-and-man sex, but this had been with an opt-out clause, with no pressure on Jake's part to go all the way unless he wanted to. And *had* he told Mark to stop, he was sure Mark would have done so.

This morning, with Tommy Vincent, Jake's bravado had seen him boasting like a man of great sexual experience—to a complete stranger. Unlike Mark, bearing in mind he was paying him an inordinately good wage to do a job that anyone in London could have done just as well if not better, Tommy would be expecting him to do *more* than he had done with Mark. Jake was sure of this. He and Mark had kissed—even this he had found strange, at first. He had loved it when Mark had rimmed him, but never in a million years would he have wanted to return the favour.

"*You don't have to look,*" Mark had told him, that first time they had fucked. "*I'll guide you. Just pretend that you're shoving it inside a fanny. There's not much difference once you get used to it.*"

Jake *hadn't* looked, but after a couple of occasions and when they had been engaged in the doggie-position, he had become *more* turned-on when looking down and watching his cock sliding in and out of the tightest, hairiest "pussy" in Christendom. And now, because of his boasting, he was starting to wonder what he might be letting himself in for.

From a callbox inside the pub entrance, he called Mark. The machine ate money with this being a long-distance call, and with the change he had in his pocket there was barely enough time to exchange pleasantries—for him to tell Mark that he was missing him already, and that Tommy Vincent had invited him around to his place.

Mark chuckled down the crackly line, "If he's invited to you to his penthouse, it'll be for one thing only. Fuck him, Jake. If it helps, close your eyes and pretend that he's me. Believe me, it'll be worth it in the long run!"

To say that Tommy Vincent's penthouse apartment was plush was an understatement. Jake had never seen such opulence extant of a glossy US television soap. Tommy answered the door—the chime, when Jake pressed the bell, was the first few bars of "Home Sweet Home." The carpet he stepped on to was ankle-deep, the walls not lined with pictures of pop singers, but what looked like genuine works of art. The furniture was genuine antique—as opposed to the ancient and worthless hand-me-down family heirlooms which cluttered every room at Partridge Farm. There were life-sized statues of near-naked Roman gods—and even a fountain in the middle of the vast living-room!

"I didn't think you'd come—no pun intended," Tommy told him. "Have you eaten?"

The fact that he was wearing a white T-shirt and skimpy tennis shorts, and barefoot, played havoc with Jake's libido. He was confident that, when it came to getting down to the nitty-gritty, his reason for being here, he would be sure not to disappoint. Wearing the same short-sleeved shirt and slacks as last night, he felt over-dressed.

Jake shook his head. He had been so apprehensive about coming here that food had been the last thing on his mind. Tommy showed him into the kitchen where there was the biggest fridge he had ever seen. Anxiously, he glanced about him.

"Who else is here, besides us?" he asked.

Tommy told him, "No one. You're perfectly safe here, Jake. And despite our comments to each other yesterday in my office, you're free to leave any time you like. I'm not going to tie you to the bed, though one or two of my boys like that kind of thing. Help yourself to some food. If all you want to do is talk, that's fine by me."

"And we both know that's not true," Jake found himself saying. "Bringing me down here and offering me thirty quid a week, when any one of hundreds of local lads would do the same job for half that. I didn't come down with the last shower, Tommy. Or should I call you boss?"

He helped himself to food from the fridge. Tommy had eaten and chose to sit opposite him and watch this strapping young man stuff his face. Jake was not the best-mannered hunk that he had brought here, and he *certainly* was not the most polite, but he was by far the most exciting. Jake was himself, no airs and graces…and no aitches, which Tommy found endearing.

He confessed, "To be honest, I don't even know *why* I suggested you coming down here. Probably it was the way

Mark described you—your plight with your old man. My own father wasn't over the moon by the way I turned out. Sexually, I mean—though he changed his tune when the cash started coming in. I told him to fuck off, and haven't seen him for nine years. I'm not sure if Mark told you the full story about us…"

"He told me nothing," Jake replied. "Well, apart from who you were and what you do. So, what *is* the story?"

For now, Tommy was not saying.

"Mark said you were the most attractive man he'd ever clapped eyes on," Tommy explained, causing Jake to colour slightly. "He's not wrong there."

He got up, fetched two bottles of beer from the fridge, and Jake could not help but notice the bulge in his shorts that had not been there ten minutes ago. Reaching across the table, Tommy took hold of Jake's paw and bunched the fingers tightly into a fist.

"I wouldn't like to be on the receiving end of that," he mused. "I suppose if it being a chauffeur doesn't work out, I could always employ you as my personal bodyguard."

Jake smiled. A week ago he had been toiling on the farm and daydreaming about Australia. Now he was going to prostitute himself to this man. There was no other way of putting it. Tommy appeared to read his mind. Getting up again, he fetched his cigarettes to the table.

"I've made a mistake," he sighed. "A *big* mistake. The job's still yours, if you want it. I shouldn't have asked you to come here. You're not like the others. It might be best if you finish your beer and I called you a cab."

Jake looked him in the eye, the way he had initially been unable to look Mark in the eye, and levelled, "I came here tonight to do a job, and I'm not leaving until I've done it."

Tommy actually seemed taken aback by Jake's candour, and Jake himself would later recall his bravado and be astonished that he could have said such a thing to someone he hardly knew. Some of Tommy's boys, before coming to work for him, had put it around like it had been going out of fashion. This man, he knew from talking to Mark, though he would never embarrass him by letting on, had little experience of sex with other men. Yet here he was making all the moves. Tommy hoped that it wasn't just cockiness, that Jake would not bottle out when push came to shove.

Taking hold of Jake's hand, Tommy led him back into the living-room, halting in front of the fountain. Standing on his tiptoes on account of their difference in height, he brushed his lips across Jake's stubbly cheeks—with there being no hot water in his room, he still had not shaved.

"So gorgeous, you make me want to cry," he murmured.

Glancing down, Jake saw how the bulge in Tommy's shorts had begun pulsating, though so far the older man's caresses were having little effect on him. Stepping back, he peeled off his T-shirt.

"So beautifully smooth," Tommy breathed. "And so perfectly sculptured. You could have been a model for one of these statues. Jupiter, with a cute Yorkshire accent…"

Tommy flicked the tip of his tongue across Jake's nipple, causing it to stiffen into a fleshy pink peak. Lifting one of Jake's long, muscular arms he licked the sweaty pit, tugging at the strong hairs with his teeth—and for Jake, strangely, it was this that caused him to stir, down below. And when Jake flexed his pecs, Tommy opted not to delay any further going for the jackpot. Sinking to his knees, he tugged at the little hairs around Jake's deeply-indented navel, and poked the point of his tongue inside. Then, unbuckling his belt, he drew the zip down and Jake's slacks collapsed about his ankles, revealing sturdy, lightly-bristled thighs. Tommy chuckled, and almost said aloud what he was thinking:

"Who wears old-fashioned Y-fronts, nowadays?"

Instead, he muttered, "You look like you might be a big lad. I guess there's only one way to find out…"

Then he decided that it might be best to slow down a bit, hoping that Jake's inexperience, as related to him by Mark—who had failed to tell him about this young man's quite phenomenal staying power—would not result in Jake hitting the jackpot before he wanted him to. Pressing his lips against the flimsy white cotton, he licked around the long diagonal bulge until it was translucent. Hooking his hands into the elasticated waistband he slowly drew down Jake's underpants, exposing the dense, glistening black pubes, and inch-by-inch the wrist-thick shaft until Jake's rock-hard weapon sprang free, slapping him under the chin.

"Fuck me," he gasped. "I know you were brought up on a farm—but are you sure you weren't sired by a horse?"

Jake smiled, and adopted the pose of a soldier, his feet slightly apart, his weapon proudly standing to attention and awaiting muster. He flinched when Tommy wrapped his fingers around his shaft and worked back his foreskin, exposing the strawberry helmet with its grinning, slightly moist slit. Running his tongue around the hardened coronal ridge, he hesitated before taking the head into his mouth—anxious that Jake might suddenly explode. When he didn't, Tommy plowed down on the rope-veined structure, taking as much of it to the back of his throat as he could without gagging. Jake dimpled his cheeks. No one had ever sucked his cock before, at least not properly. Mark never had, and one woman had tried, but in doing so had almost thrown up. And this felt *indescribably* good, this first ever gorging of his meat while Tommy's other hand gently massaged his scrotum, rolling his big balls around in their increasingly tightening sack.

"Better be careful," Jake groaned. "You're going to end up making me fetch before I want to…"

Tommy regurgitated the tasty log and chuckled at Jake's quaint terminology. Untying his shoes, he removed these and his socks, then helped Jake step out of his slacks and Y-fronts. Standing up, and moving back a pace, he admired the view. Naked and standing in front of the tinkling fountain, this young man looked far lovelier than *any* Roman god. None of the others—and there had been a great many—had been possessed of such brazen beauty and been unaware of the fact, as this perfect specimen seemingly was!

Jake was eager to get on with the party—intrigued by the bulge in Tommy's shorts which looked like it had a life of its own. He had enjoyed being undressed and having his cock sucked, and though he wanted to undress Tommy, something he and Mark had never done to each other, he was unsure about going down on him, if Tommy was expecting him to return the compliment.

"I want to see you naked," he rapped, more by way of a command than a request, and which thrilled Tommy, who preferred his men to be dominant, but had rarely found any of his conquests to be so.

Tommy removed his T-shirt, and Jake caught his breath as he had that day in the turnip field. Tommy was no less hirsute than Mark had been, save that the jet-black carpet covering his entire upper half was neatly-trimmed. He lost the shorts, and underneath was wearing white silk briefs which clearly defined the outline of his erection. Turning around, he slowly lowered his undies, revealing tight cheeks which surprisingly were almost hairless. Then he executed a pirouette and faced Jake once more, his sturdy, cut seven-incher jutting out at a right-angle to his trimmed pubes. Jake swallowed hard. He had come this far and there would be no backing out now.

"Lovely," he breathed. "You don't have a foreskin like everybody else…"

Tommy chuckled, "Jewish men don't, sweetheart. Does that bother you?"

"Not at all," Jake replied. "So long as it works…"

Tommy moved towards him. Their lips brushed, as did the tips of their cocks. Then Tommy bent his downwards and slid it between Jake's thighs so that he could dry-hump his scrotum—flinching as the bristles of the younger man's perineum prickled his rod. And when a few minutes later Tommy stopped frigging his nut-sack and stood back, Jake observed that it was still dry.

"Promise me summat," Jake murmured. "Promise you won't fetch in my mouth."

Tommy had never heard the term before, and Jake had said it twice tonight.

"Cross my heart," he replied, as Jake squatted on his haunches in front of him, making his thighs look even more massive, while his big cock pressed flat against his abs.

He didn't suck on the small, shell-pink helmet for very long or, he suspected, as well as he should have done. This was all new to him, and he simply wanted to find out what a man's cock tasted like. Now he knew, and it tasted *good*!

"I think we'd better go into the bedroom," Tommy said, coaxing him to his feet—not wishing to hurt Jake's feelings by telling him it was customary, when giving a blow-job, not to be too rough with one's teeth.

The bedroom was no less opulent than everything else in the penthouse—a large circular bed draped with white satin and with a large towel spread across the middle. Tommy had obviously anticipated this moment. Lying face-down on the towel, he spread his thighs wide. Then he looked up at Jake, whose eyes were taking in the whole room as if he had lost something.

"Where's the Vaseline," he asked, in a little voice.

Tommy told him, "The blue tube on top of the drawers. Vaseline went out with the Ark, sweetheart. Don't use too much of it, though, otherwise you might keep slipping out."

Reaching behind him with both hands, he spread his cakes. Jake had expected his crack to be as hairy as the rest of him but the entire trench—from the puckered bud to the back of his scrotum—had been shaved smooth as an egg.

Mark had always "greased" himself up, but Jake figured that he would have to do the job himself. Squeezing a large blob of lubricant on to his finger—this certainly felt better than dipping it into the tub of Vaseline—he applied it to Tommy's tight-looking hole. As he did this, Tommy raised his rump up off the mattress, and Jake realised that here was one rectum that he would not be able to slide straight into. Moments ago, he had sucked a cock for the first time. Now there was another first as he squeezed more lubricant from the tube on to his finger, poked this inside Tommy's chute, and wiggled it around. Tommy seemed to like this. It certainly opened him up and, satisfied that he would get in there without splitting him down the middle, Jake knelt between Tommy's thighs, and pushed his helmet inside the gaping chasm. Tommy groaned loudly, but as these were groans of pleasure and not discomfort, Jake relaxed his full weight on top of him, and fed him all nine inches.

Grasping Tommy's waist, and with Tommy once more raising himself up off the mattress to meet him, thrust by thrust, Jake kept up a steady movement for a good fifteen minutes—hardly the actions of a novice, the older man told himself as the big gonads slapped back and forth against his own. Then, he suddenly stopped moaning.

"I think you'd better pull out, baby…"

71

Jake did so at once, and got off the bed.

"I'm sorry," he began. "I didn't mean to hurt you…"

"*Hurt* me?" Tommy grinned. "You're not *hurting* me, Jake. I just want to look at that lovely face of yours while you're *fetching*, as you call it."

Rolling on to his back, he scissored his legs high into the air. Wedging his big frame between them, Jake sank inside him once more and decided, despite his lack of experience, that this would probably always be his preferred position, the one he adopted when having sex with women so that he could suck their tits once he got down to the short strokes. For a few minutes more he seesawed back and forth, every now and then withdrawing completely and waiting a few seconds before plunging back in, each deep stab bringing him closer towards his climax while Tommy masturbated himself in perfect rhythm to each stroke until his sphincter tightened its grip on him, making it impossible for Jake to hold back any longer. Screwing his eyes shut and clenching his teeth, Jake prepared himself for blast-off.

"Quick," Tom rapped. "Pull out and shoot all over me. Don't waste it by shooting it inside my arse. I want to watch you come!"

Jake withdrew, with seconds to spare, arched his back and thrust his hips forwards, and let rip with half a dozen copious silver streamers which criss-crossed Tommy's abdomen and chest. Then, as he was thinking of pushing his cock back inside him and starting all over again, Tommy yelled for him to get off the bed and get on his knees. Unsure of what he had in mind and still reeling from his massive climax, Jake complied.

"Hold your head up, baby," he panted, wanking like a man possessed. "Look into my eyes…"

Seconds later, Jake recoiled as though hit at point-blank range by a shower of white-hot arrows as Tommy blasted his load across his chest, and shuddered as the semen began trickling between his sweat-streaked pecs, south towards his pubes. Thoroughly spent, but only for now, Tommy toppled backwards on to the bed.

"Jake Nelson," he announced. "Welcome to Thomas J Vincent Enterprises. You're now officially a member of the T J V Fuck Club!"

5: Lennie

July 1964

It was a relief to be getting out of the scruffy digs. Last night, Jake had slept at Tommy's penthouse, comfortably in his bed, and though they had not had sex again, Jake had wanted them to. Since discovering this new physical world, he was starting to wonder if he would ever have sex with a woman again—indeed, not sure that he ever wanted to, for what he had experienced so far with other men exceeded anything he had done with any of the women back home.

Back home, if he had seen an attractive woman in the street he had told himself, "Wow, I wouldn't mind slipping *her* a length—great tits and legs!"

Mark had suggested that he might be a "double-blade", but Jake was not so sure. Since Mark, things had changed and he was past asking himself why, if an attractive *man* passed him in the street—especially one wearing tight crotch-revealing trousers, or one with bulging muscles—he was now thinking himself, and once out loud, causing the man in question to swiftly turn around, "I wouldn't mind sticking my cock inside *his* arse and making *him* fetch!"

He was learning more, *experimenting* more, with each new day! Last night, albeit briefly, he had sucked a cock! He had let a man shoot his spunk down his chest! This morning, he had awoken with a hard-on, and Tommy had flung back the sheets and told him to relax, close his eyes, and let it all go. Wrapped around his tool, Tommy's hand had felt like a mink glove, Jake had blown a load with such gusto that it had made his ears pop. He had completely drenched Tommy's fist, but Tommy had not even got hard while bringing him off. And afterwards, Tommy had licked his fingers clean! Jake wondered if he would ever be capable of doing *that*! He doubted it—but then again, a few weeks ago he would never have dreamed of *kissing* a man, let alone of doing other things with him!

"I'm afraid I'm not a morning person," Tommy told him while they were driving across London to pick up Jake's things. "But don't think for one moment think that last night was a one off, because it wasn't."

Jake found it amusing—the boss driving the chauffeur around—and after dropping him off, Tommy told him to "report to base" at three. The new digs were near Oxford Circus, within walking distance of Tommy's office, not much bigger than the one he had vacated, but better appointed and immaculately clean. The double bed was in an alcove separated from the main room, and there was a kitchenette and a bathroom with a tub *and* shower. There was also a phone—Tommy stressed for making local calls only, that should Jake wish to call long-distance he would have to pay, which would still be cheaper than a callbox. Every Monday, he added, a woman collected the laundry.

"And how much is everything going to cost?" Jake had asked him. "My name's Nelson, not Rothschild."

Tommy had told him, "The rent and laundry's part and parcel of your salary, so you don't have to pay anything. Well—a little time with that gorgeous body and big cock of yours won't go amiss."

75

Jake had chuckled at this and responded, "I think that can be arranged."

The first think he did was have a shower and shave. Then he thought about what he should put on for this afternoon, when he assumed he would be meeting the esteemed Lennie Stevens. He realised that he didn't have much to wear other than the black slacks and white shirt he had worn since arriving in London—the latter now in need of washing. There was a little café near where he was staying. He ate here, and afterwards visited a department store where he dipped into his father's wallet and bought a black jacket and slacks, underwear and socks, and a pale blue shirt. He considered buying a tie, but changed his mind. It was too warm for ties.

Jake's first meeting with Lennie Stevens did not get off to a good start. He had heard him on the radio and seen him many times on the television, and had found his music very bland. He recalled what Tommy had said, about some of these singers not being able to hold a note, and of how the recording studio technicians made them sound better than they did on stage.

Lennie turned up late. He was in his late-twenties and shorter than Jake had anticipated, around the same height as Tommy and barely reaching past his shoulders. He was wearing denims and a short-sleeve checked cowboy shirt, and around his neck a chain with some sort of medallion. He *was* fairly muscular and certainly good-looking with a squarish jaw, angular cheekbones, big brown eyes, and a shock of greased, light-brown hair, teased into a Billy Fury quiff. His teeth were slightly crooked but he only showed these when he smiled, which was not often—in keeping with his trademark moody image. The accent was Welsh.

Tommy introduced them, "Jake, this is Lennie. Lennie—meet your new chauffeur."

Jake stuck out his hand, "Pleased to meet you, Lennie."

The other man frowned as he pronounced, "Actually, it's *sir* to you, boyo."

Jake was not sure if he was joking, but told him just the same, "I've never called anybody sir in my life, and I'm not going to start doing so now."

The singer raised his bushy eyebrows. Like his hair these were greased.

"Looks like we're going to get along fine—better than the last retard I had," he said. "So long as you remember who's boss—"

"Which happens to be me," Tommy interjected. "Behave yourself, Lennie. And it's a quarter-to-four. You should've been at the photo shoot twenty minutes ago."

Tommy handed Jake a sheet of paper with instructions how to get to the photographer's studio, and he followed Lennie down the stairs and out into the street. A group of female fans were clustered on the pavement. They screamed Lennie's name and rushed forward with their autograph books. Lennie ignored them—indeed, he stuck his nose in the air—and headed for the white Rolls-Royce parked fifty yards away. Instead of getting into the car, he stood by the door waiting for Jake to open it. Jake decided there and then that he would probably never like this man.

"Bloody silly females get on my nerves," he said, as Jake started up the engine. "I had one woman send me her knickers through the post. She wanted me to come in them and send them back, the dirty cow. They're all cows. Where are you from, Jake? Are you a Yorkshireman? I never did meet one yet who could talk properly."

"Yorkshire and proud of the fact," Jake retorted. "You're Welsh right? Don't they shag sheep and goats where you come from?"

"From the valleys, and equally proud of the fact," Lennie told him, with a grin. "One of Tommy's very rare failures, in the bedroom department. I suppose he's told you all about that?"

Jake shook his head, though Tommy *had* told him, and concentrated on the busy road ahead. Lennie then asked him point-blank if *he* was a homosexual. He shook his head once more, and reminded himself that he was getting rather good at telling fibs.

"Thank goodness for that," Lennie responded. "My last driver was queer *and* a Jehovah's Witness, always spouting claptrap from the Bible and saying how we sinners are going to face eternal damnation. Then off he'd go and stick it up his boyfriend's rear end. Do you go to church, Jake?"

"Only to weddings and funerals," he replied, drily.

They pulled up outside the photographer's studio, a large, grimy-looking terraced house near Covent Garden. Lennie remained in the passenger seat until Jake got out of the car to open the door.

"He thinks I'm his skivvy," he thought to himself. "I can't see this lasting long."

He began following Lennie into the building, but a glare from the singer and a sharp nod towards the expensive car told him that his place was with the Rolls. There was a kiosk nearby and he bought a newspaper, then returned to the car. Between reading his paper and watching the comings and goings to the photographic studio through the rear-view mirror, he reflected on his adventure thus far.

Sex with Tommy Vincent had been exciting—even the wank this morning in the most opulent surroundings he had ever seen. And Tommy had suggested that there was more to come. Jake was still worried about Mark, of how he might be coping two-hundred miles away and unemployed, at the mercy of the village gossips. He also could not help but wonder about the "scandal" that had seen Mark fleeing from London up to Yorkshire, and what this might have to do with Tommy. Then his thoughts turned to Ricky, the man he had met in the pub the other night. A Dilly Boy, he had called himself—in other words, a prostitute. The ones Jake had seen back home—in Doncaster outside the Black Bull—had all looked rough as hell. One had propositioned him once, and told him that for just ten shillings she could take him to heaven and back.

He had told her, resulting in a torrent of abuse not just from her but from her colleagues, "Why waste ten-bob on an old boot like you when I can have a wank for nothing and know where my fingers have been?"

It had never crossed his mind that men might do this sort

79

of thing for a living too. Ricky had not looked rough at all, and Jake was wondering how much it would cost to go with such a man when he glanced up at the mirror and observed Lennie, walking towards the car. There was no denying that Lennie was cute, but he was arrogant. He had made it clear that he disliked Northerners and homosexuals, and what he had said about women suggested that he did not care much for them, either. He had denounced his last driver as a retard, which Jake found inexcusable.

"We'll see how things go," he told himself. "If he thinks I'm getting out to open the door, he can think again."

Lennie got into the car. His shirt was open to the waist, revealing a pleasant expanse of dusky chest hair. He noticed Jake looking at this.

"Are you *sure* you're not a homo?" he pressed.

Jake felt that he had nothing to lose, that if push came to shove he could get out of the car, and leave this obnoxious individual to make his own way home.

"You could always try touching me up," he suggested. "Then you'd find out for sure, wouldn't you?"

Lennie glanced at the fists gripping the wheel, twice the size of his own, and decided to say no more. He gave Jake instructions how to get to Mayfair, then asked him to stop the car, adding that he would walk the rest of the way.

"I reckon I'm going to like you, Jake," he said. "You've got guts, buddy."

And Jake told himself, as he watched him march away with his nose in the air, "I can assure you the feeling's not mutual, *buddy*!"

Jake drove back to Tommy Vincent's office, and handed the keys to the man who looked after this car and Tommy's Bentley. He walked back to his digs, where he changed, and went out to eat. He thought about heading for Soho and finishing the evening off at the Golden Lion. Then he changed his mind, called at an off-licence and bought six bottles of beer, and took these back to his room where he spent the rest of the evening watching the television.

The next morning, wearing his more comfortable attire of denims and white T-shirt, Jake breakfasted at a greasy spoon, then walked the short distance to Tommy Vincent's office. It was sunny, and the streets were bustling with dolly-birds…and whatever their male equivalents were called in this part of the world. Never in his life had he seen so many tight arses and bulging crotches, and these played havoc with his libido. The receptionist—her name was Sheila, and today she was not wearing a hat—let him in and told him that Mr. Vincent needed to see him at once. Jake had a pretty good idea why, as he tapped on the door and Tommy shouted for him to come in. He was wearing dark grey chinos, a short-sleeve candy-stripe shirt, and sitting behind his desk in a swivel chair.

"I know what you're going to say," Jake gruffed. "Your precious Mr. Stevens doesn't like me. The feeling's mutual. He's so bloody rude—had he been anybody else, I'd have belted him one for some of the things he said yesterday."

Tommy smiled and said, "Actually, that's where you're wrong. Lenny *does* like you, he says because you speak your mind and don't take any shit. It's always taken a brave man to stand up to that feisty little prima donna. If his girlie fans knew what he was really like, they'd give him a suitably wide berth."

"Then why put up with him?" Jake asked. "And why did you want to see me urgently?"

Tommy enlightened him, "In answer to question number one, I put up with Lennie because he earns me more money than all the others added together."

He got up, crossed the room, and dropped the latch on the door.

"And in answer to question number two…"

Jake recalled what Tommy had said during their first meeting—about bending him over his desk—and his heart began beating fast. Surely he was not expecting them to do the business here, when there were half-a-dozen people in the office on the other side of the door?"

Tommy strode up to him, and gave him a peck on the lips. Kneeling in front of him, he unzipped Jake's denims and pulled them over his thighs and to his below his knees.

"Thank God you've ditched those boring Y-fronts," he murmured, as he pressed his lips against the big mound in Jake's bright blue cotton briefs, and their contents responded accordingly.

Time was of the essence, and Tommy drew these down, freeing Jake's massive cock. Grasping the rope-veined shaft with its pronounced spunk-pipe with one hand, he gently worked back the foreskin several times, exposing the beautiful strawberry cap and then making it disappear again inside its fleshy hood. Working the tip of his tongue inside this, he was amazed at its elasticity. Without exception, all the stars he had bedded had foreskins, but none of them as tactile as this one. He held it back over the coronal ridge, and Jake clenched his cheeks as Tommy worked his magic on the tangle of nerves beneath the vee. Reaching under Jake's scrotum with his other hand, Tommy located his rectum, still damp and easily accessible after his morning shower. Jake shuddered as two very rough fingers worked their way past his sphincter to explore the warm, tight channel. Then, as his fingers explored a little deeper, easily locating Jake's prostate, so he plowed all the way down on the turgid log, taking a good half of it to the back of his throat. He almost had Jake where he wanted him when the phone shrilled, bringing them back to reality.

"Don't you *dare* move," Tommy rapped, reaching across to grab the receiver, still keeping his fingers deep-rooted in Jake's arse.

It was Lennie Stevens. Jake heard every word, saying he was on his way to the office, and hoping that Jake was there to drive him to the recording studio.

"You caught me bang in the middle of a late breakfast," Tommy told him, impatiently. "Jake hasn't come yet, but he shouldn't be too long."

He put down the receiver, and resumed fellating—while Jake cursed Lennie Stevens under his breath. Tommy had taken an enormous risk, doing what he was doing now, but Jake really *had* been hoping that he might risk taking things further, bearing in mind that those rough fingers had done a sterling job opening him up.....that there was no better time than now for Tommy to fulfil his promise to bend him over his desk so that they could come together, instead of the sex being so one-sided as it had been yesterday morning. On the plus side, Tommy *had* unbuttoned his shirt so that Jake was able to look down and feast his eyes on his sublimely hairy chest while being sucked off. Then, as Tommy went down on him just a little further and those two expert fingers became three, Jake's eyes suddenly crossed over the bridge of his nose as he bucked his hips and thrashed his salty load past Tommy's tonsils. His senses were buzzing, but even though he was done Tommy kept on sucking hard until assured he had devoured every last droplet of man-juice.

"Just what the doctor ordered," he pronounced, getting to his feet and wiping his mouth with the back of his hand. "My protein quota for the day."

Jake pulled up his briefs, and put his tackle away.

"It's so unfair," he said, zipping up his denims. "That's twice you've done me, and twice I've not done you back."

Tommy chuckled, "You will. Don't worry your pretty head about that. But I've got Tony Milano coming round after lunch—if you get my drift."

Jake understood. He figured it must have been a tough regime having to shag all those handsome men—even those who might have been as unpleasant as Lennie Stevens.

Lennie was waiting for him in the outside office. He was wearing his "recording gear"—his lucky powder-blue silk tracksuit with his name emblazoned across the back, and a white baseball cap—perched on top of his quiff, which Jake thought made him look effeminate. He imagined what the reaction would be, should he venture out into a Yorkshire street looking the way he did right now.

The studios were in Maida Vale. Lennie rapped out orders how to get here, and when Jake pulled up in the car-park and leaned across him to open the passenger door, the singer gave his arm a squeeze.

"I could be in here for hours," he said. "Hand the keys in at the office. The concierge will see that it's parked. Then come upstairs and enjoy the experience without having to buy a ticket."

"The experience?" Jake posed, then the penny dropped.

"You'll get to meet Martha," Lennie added. "She's my lady—well, for this week. The best cock-sucker in London. Play your cards right, boyo, and I might put in a good word for you."

Jake chuckled to himself, and wondered what Lennie would say if he told him, "If you want your cock sucking, *boyo*, look no further than your manager. He sucked me off half an hour ago and my ears are still ringing!"

As a vocalist, Jake found Lennie Stevens unbelievably dire, and recalled what Tommy had said about technicians making some of these people sound better than they really were. The song—or blockbuster ballad, as Lennie described it—was "Let Me Be The Man Of Your Dreams", written by Lennie, and Jake was sure that few of his female fans, the ones who had screamed at him yesterday and those who were so infatuated that they sent him their panties through the post, might not *want* him to be the man

85

of their dreams if they knew that he regarded most of them as cows. Jake was still reeling over what Lennie had said about homosexuals, calling them retards. Back home he had rarely heard anything positive said about homosexuals, and felt guilty that he may have even occasionally frowned upon them himself, until becoming one.

The song itself was not bad, Jake considered. The lyrics were banal, as were those of most songs in the pop charts— the sort that a child could write with comparative ease—but the tune was catchy, and the trio of girl backing singers made it easier on the ear. It was not just that Lennie's voice was so loud, but tuneless! Jake was sure he could have done better and he had always deemed himself tone-deaf!

The first hitch occurred when Lennie stopped during the first take and yelled at the sound man for giving him too much bass. Three takes later, he was moaning that he did not like the way one of the musicians kept staring at him.

Jake could have marched up to him and hit him when he bawled at the producer, "I've told you before, Larry, I don't want any fucking queers accompanying me and putting me off. My arse is not up for grabs. Either he goes, or I do."

Sitting in a darkened corner of the studio, Jake shook his head in disbelief as the musician unplugged his guitar and walked off. There were at least another ten takes, by which time the song was really starting to get on Jake's nerves.

Then at last, the producer shouted, "That's it! We're all done, boys!"

Panting and perspiring, Lennie joined Jake and asked him what he thought about his new song—then not waiting for an answer responded to his own question, "It's brilliant, of course. Maybe not the *best* I've ever done, but it'll get into the Top Five, at least. God, singing makes me feel *so* horny. Which reminds me…"

He stuck two fingers between his lips and whistled, as if calling a dog. One of the backing singers—Jake later found out that she also worked as a model for one of London's top fashion designers—came tripping across the room, balanced precariously on the highest heels Jake had ever seen. She was wearing a pink mini-skirt and a matching low-cut blouse which barely contained her massive breasts. She and Lennie rubbed noses, like Eskimos, and he introduced them.

"Martha—this is chauffeur, my driver. Jake—this is my girl Martha, the wettest pussy in London."

Martha giggled, and tossed back her long blonde hair. She was pretty, exactly the type Jake might have fancied in the "old" days. They shook hands, and Martha eyed him up and down as if sizing up a prize stallion at an auction—then audaciously grabbed a handful.

"What a big boy you are," she chirped, giving the goods a lingering squeeze which soon proved to Jake that he had not lost his libido where females were concerned. "Tell me Jake—are you big all over?"

Jake was lost for words, embarrassed that he had started to develop a semi, and that this was clearly visible by way of the sizeable bulge in his denims.

Lennie nodded towards this, saw how the colour rushed

to Jake's cheeks and told him, "Don't be bashful, boyo. Martha only has to look at a man and he's hard as rock in ten seconds flat. Come on, we'd better get going."

Martha giggled all the way to the car. She was all over Lennie during the drive to Mayfair. Jake half-expected them to start having sex in the back of the Rolls, and was dreading that if this happened, having observed his excited state these two might ask him to join in. He had always hated giddy girls, and the thought of watching Lennie and Martha through the rear-view mirror, doubtless with Lennie giving a running commentary, made him feel ill at ease. Lennie asked him to stop the car at exactly the same spot as the day before, and when he got out indicated the bulge made by his very pronounced erection.

"I swear to God, I'm going to have to whip it out and get her to make me shoot *before* I get to the house," he told Jake. "It'll not be the first time I've had to take a girl into a back-alley for a quickie up against the wall. London's full of dolly-birds like Martha who are gagging for it. Would you believe, I've never had *one* wank in over three years?"

With this, he strolled off, Martha trotting behind him like a lackey.

"Just what I needed to know," Jake muttered to himself. "What an arrogant arsehole!"

After leaving the car at the garage, Jake bought a snack from a delicatessen and headed for his digs. He had started to develop a headache on account of the raucous music that had assaulted his ears most of the morning. After lunch he took a nap, hoping that this might make him feel better, but when he awoke his headache was worse. He showered, and was settling down to watch the television before having an early night when Tommy called to inform him that Lennie and Martha had left town for a few days—in the singer's words "to fuck their brains out"—and that they would not be back until Monday afternoon. Tommy told Jake to report to the office first thing Tuesday morning. Thomas Vincent Enterprises was putting together its early autumn tour. Tommy added that as Lennie felt it beneath him to travel on the coach with everyone else, Jake would be driving him around the country.

"The mind boggles," he mused to himself, after Tommy hung up. "It's bad enough driving him around here for just a few minutes, without having him in the back of the bloody car for hours on end!"

6: Ricky

July 1964

Jake spent the next day, Saturday, visiting tourist haunts: St Paul's Cathedral, Buckingham Palace, and Marble Arch. At eight after eating in Chinatown he ended up at an almost empty Golden Lion, where he found "Dilly Boy" Ricky not leaning against the bar, but working behind it. He came around to Jake's side of the counter, and they shook hands.

"This is a nice surprise," Ricky beamed. "Never thought I'd see you in here again, looking fit as a butcher's dog."

Jake had made no special effort to dress up, as he might have back home where it was almost traditional for young men to go out on a weekend wearing smart trousers, jacket and shirt, and maybe a tie. He *was* wearing his black slacks, but had eschewed his shirt for a tight-fitting white T-shirt he had bought from a market stall that morning.

Neither was Ricky what Jake would consider "dressed for business", as he had been last Tuesday. He was wearing scuffed denims, sneakers, and a navy-blue T-shirt.

"Night off?" Jake asked.

Ricky ran his fingers through his long blond locks and explained, "Trade's been slack these last few days. The boys are scared of venturing out. There was a murder in Regent's Park, Tuesday. One of the cruising areas. I sometimes go there if there's nothing doing around Soho, or if I fancy a change of scenery. Not any more, though."

Jake pressed him for more details but he seemed reticent to talk about it, so he changed the subject to more mundane topics: the hot weather, his visit earlier to Carnaby Street where he had seen men and women dressed in clothes most of the folk back home would not be seen dead in.

"Home," he told Ricky. "It sounds weird saying that now because I don't feel that I *have* a home any more—just a rather nice room with a few mod-cons near Oxford Circus. I'd forgotten what it's like to cook my own tea—well, they call it dinner here, and what we call dinner in Yorkshire, you people call lunch. And the beer's so bloody expensive, like everything else."

At ten, twenty-five minutes before last orders, Jack—the landlord whose halitosis had almost floored Jake during his last visit here—arrived to take over the bar and cash up, and Jake and Ricky took their drinks to a table. Ricky could not help but stare at the slab of beefcake sitting opposite him, his fleshy nipples outlined through the flimsy fabric of his T-shirt, but most especially at those full, kissable lips. He was wondering if Jake might be big all over—and what his reaction might be should he reach across and run his fingers through that lovely thick shock of dark hair when Jake's melodious voice cut into his lecherous thoughts.

"So, who's been murdered? Is it somebody you know?"

"Probably," Ricky shrugged. "All we know so far is that he was male. I always thought Regent's was safe. Much safer than cruising Hampstead Heath, that's for sure."

Jake was learning something new every day. The only cruising he had heard of until now took place on a ship, though he wasn't going to show his ignorance by telling Ricky this. He asked him if the profession paid well.

"Up in Yorkshire the asking price outside the Black Bull —that's a bag shanty near Doncaster cattle-market—is seven-and-six," he explained. "My uncle went with one of them once and ended up giving his missus the clap."

The light grey eyes flashed at this, and Ricky told him, keeping his voice to a raised whisper, "It's different with us Dilly Boys. Very few of us allow the punters to go all the way. I've never gone all the way in all the years I've been doing trade. A lot of them are married and they don't want to end up like your uncle, catching something and passing it on to their wives. So it's hand jobs and blowies. Usually it's half-a-crown, but if the punter looks loaded, it's ten-bob."

"And how many…punters…are there in a night?" Jake enquired.

Ricky dipped into the pocket of his denims for his du Maurier cigarettes, and offered one to Jake.

"That depends," he said. "Two, sometimes three or four. In the tourist season there can be as many as ten. Why so inquisitive, Jake? Are you wanting to buy? You told me the other night you didn't fancy me."

"Just curious," Jake replied. "I've never met anyone like you before. But—how do you manage to fetch *ten* times in one night? Doesn't it make your cock sore?"

Ricky guffawed, and the pub's few customers turned and stared—Jake had pronounced this louder than he should.

"I don't *come* at all," he said. "Well, only if the bloke's very special. Otherwise I let them fiddle with me while I'm tossing them off. They usually finish before I even start getting turned on. I make sure of that if it's some old bloke. Then I go home and have my supper."

They finished their drinks and got up to leave. Jake was astonished how, so soon after shouting time, the bar staff down here collected the glasses and almost pushed you out of the door—not like back home where you could take your time. He followed Ricky out into the street, thronging with people because the theatres were turning out.

"It doesn't have to end here," Ricky said, as a gentle breeze whipped his golden locks about his face. "We could go to a club—or back to mine if you've changed your mind about not fancying me."

Jake pondered over this. The lanky blond was cute, and he *did* fancy him. But all that talk about homosexuals being bumped off in parks made him suspicious of accompanying anyone to a place he was unfamiliar with, besides which he had an inkling that Ricky might live in some scruffy bedsit like the dump *he* had stayed in when arriving in London, approached by some dimly-lit back alley where anything could happen. And though he looked clean enough, Jake was thinking that if he *was* going to have sex with this man, then maybe a shower would not go amiss, just to be sure.

"I've a better idea," he said. "Why don't *you* come back to *my* place?"

On the corner of Rupert Street, Ricky flagged down a cab. Jake recalled Lennie and Martha, how they had been all over each other like a rash in the back of the Rolls, and he was hoping Ricky would not do the same, particularly as

93

he goosed him as they were leaving the pub. The last thing he wanted was to be arrested for lewd behaviour in the back of a taxi. In fact, Ricky sat two feet away from him and never moved until they reached Oxford Circus, when to Jake's surprise he took out his wallet and paid the driver.

Likewise when they got to Jake's room, Ricky seemed reluctant to make the first move. Jake had re-stocked the fridge. He made ham sandwiches, which they washed down with a shared bottle of beer.

"So," Jake posed. "Now that nobody's listening, what's all this about somebody getting bumped off in the park?"

As the words died on his lips, he felt it a strange question to be asking someone with whom he was about to get intimate—but felt he had to say something to keep the chat going, as Ricky had seemingly gone all shy on him.

"Like I said, there's not much to tell," he replied. "When the weather's nice some of us like to spread our wings. Off we fly to Hampstead Heath, or Clapham Common. That's where all the lonely blokes go, or the ones who don't want their wives and girlfriends to find out they like cock."

"Where it's easy to get nabbed by the bobbies, I don't doubt," Jake put in. "Have you ever been nabbed, Jake?"

He shook his head, "No. On the Heath or the Common there's usually a copper hanging around— keeping his eyes peeled, looking forward to getting a blowie at the end of his shift. A couple of detectives came into the pub this lunchtime, making routine enquiries. All they said was that a man's body had been found in Regent's Park. It didn't take much working out he was a homo, buying or selling. If not they wouldn't have come to the Lion."

Jake had finished his sandwich, and Ricky had swigged the last of his beer. There were other bottles in the fridge, but Jake was eager to get on with things, albeit that he was feeling nervous, this being the first time he had brought a man home, so to speak. Raising one arm, he sniffed his pit and feigned disgust.

"I stink sweaty," he said. "I'm going to have a shower. Care to join me?"

Ricky removed his shoes and socks, and followed Jake into the bathroom, the plushest he had ever seen.

"Nice," he said. "I'm not used to this sort of luxury."

"Me neither," Jake returned, kicking off his own shoes and removing his socks. "At the farm, until I was ten we had a tin tub hanging on the wall outside in the yard. The old man dragged it into the kitchen, Mother boiled water in the copper, and muggins here was always last in. Wouldn't want to go back to those days, that's for sure."

For a moment they stood facing each other, each waiting for the other to make the first move. Jake assumed that as a so-called "Dilly Boy", Ricky would not be expecting the kind of sex he'd had with Mark and Tommy. He only hoped that he wouldn't want to do anything kinky. What he didn't know was that Ricky was apprehensive too. Sex for him, extant of a relationship, had always been hurried—you didn't take your time on the Heath or in one of the parks, you just wanted to get the punter off before someone tapped you on the shoulder. And this man was different from the others. He was not the sort who would pay for it—

95

or even go looking for it in gaffs like the Golden Lion. He knew Jake's ending up there had been purely by chance. All the better for him, of course!

Then Jake peeled off his T-shirt, and Ricky caught his breath. This man had a *cleavage*! He had fleshy, pointed nipples the size of half-crowns that you could hang your hat on! Ricky's last "conquest" had been in his fifties, with a beer belly and breath like boiling cabbage. He had handed over the customary ten-shillings and Ricky had taken him around the back of the Cambridge Theatre, ostensibly to suck him off. The man's cock had smelled so cheesy and rank that he had almost gagged. Standing up, he had tossed him off and given him five-shillings back. Now he chuckled to himself at the thought of Jake going on the game—and putting all the other boys out of business.

"You've got amazing tits," he enthused, moving towards him, having decided that if one of them was going to get things going, it would have to be him.

"Nobody's ever told me that before," Jake murmured, as their lips collided.

This was still new to him. Mark he knew had experience, Tommy certainly so. But this was different. He was about to get his rocks off with a sex worker, and knew that he would to have to put in an exemplary performance. Ricky did not sense this comparative lack of experience as he sucked hard on one nipple, then the other while one hand cupped Jake's crotch. Descending slowly, he poked the tip of his tongue inside the deeply-indented navel, then tugged at the little hairs surrounding it. Unbuckling Jake's belt, he drew down his zip and helped him step out of his denims. Pressing his lips against the huge bulge in his cotton briefs, he inhaled deeply, savouring the heady aroma of farm boy on heat. His heart was pounding, wondering if Jake's cock would be as beautiful and in proportion to the rest of him. Then he let out a loud gasp as he pulled down his undies, and observed that it was.

"Gorgeous cock," he breathed. "Gorgeous balls. In fact, everything about you is so fucking gorgeous that it makes me want to cry."

Standing up, Ricky stepped back a few paces, and slowly undressed. Pulling his T-shirt over his head, he revealed a pleasantly muscular chest, the pecs divided by an attractive fan of honey-coloured bristles. Turning his back on Jake, he sashayed his hips like a hula-hula dancer as he lowered his denims. He was wearing nothing underneath, and Jake's cock twitched as its owner marvelled at the smooth, firm cheeks, the sturdy thighs, the long, surprisingly hairy legs.

"Beautiful," he murmured. "Absolutely lovely…"

Ricky turned around, his long fingers spread wide over his crotch, concealing the goods. He had tucked his cock under his thighs so that when he removed his hands and extended his arms, cruciform, he looked like a woman with an exceedingly hairy pussy. Jake stared at the lush honey thicket, not quite sure what he was seeing, what he might have been letting himself in for—but not giving a damn because he really, *really* wanted to shove his cock inside this delectable creature.

"You like, baby?" Ricky teased, effecting a poor French accent. "You want to sample *zee* goods?"

Jake liked a lot, and he was thinking to himself, "I don't give a rat's arse if you're a he, a she, or summat in between. All I know is I'm going to fuck you senseless, and when I've done fucking you senseless, I'm going to fuck you senseless again."

Then, while he was still staring, Ricky opened his legs and his cock sprang free and slapped back against his belly, bouncing up and down several times like a diving-board before settling at right-angles to his pubes—*ten* inches of wrist-thick meat, sturdy and uncut, weighted down by a massive, almost smooth boxer's glove scrotum.

"Fuck me," he muttered.

"That's *zee* idea, baby," Ricky purred, still effecting the French accent. "Though tonight, for you, I am more than willing to be versatile."

Jake stepped into the cubicle and switched on the taps. For several minutes they stood under the spray, enveloped in steam and soaping one another down, cocks slapping together like duellists' swords. Several times they kissed, and for the first time Jake enjoyed the experience of having a man's tongue in his mouth. Then when the suds had been rinsed away, Ricky moved behind him to nuzzle the nape of his neck, wedging his big log between Jake's thighs so that the glans was mashed against his perineum. Ricky felt sure that if he stayed like this for long enough he would offload even without moving—but he had more exciting things in mind. Working his way downwards he kissed Jake all the way down his spine, his stubble biting into the delicate flesh until he reached his tailbone.

"You like, *monsewer?*" he posed.

Jake's groans were his only response as Ricky slid two fingers inside him—stretching and periscoping more gently than Tommy had, and very soon locating his prostate. The sensation was like nothing Jake had ever felt before. Mark had had his cock up there, but even that had not felt as good as this Dilly Boy's fingers. Then, withdrawing his digits and spreading Jake's cheeks wide, Ricky plunged his face into the furry crack as the water plastered his hair to his head. Jake squirmed as the tip of Ricky's tongue progressed through the hard ring of muscle. Such was the pleasure that he badly needed to reach down and start wanking, but was unable to do so because the flats of both his hands were pressed hard against the tiles in front of him for support. He knew what was coming next. It was not what he had planned, but the last thing he wanted was for Ricky to stop.

"Are you ready for the big event?" Ricky demanded, now back to his Cockney accent."

"As ready as I'll ever be," he mused, as Ricky rose to his feet, turned off the shower and pushed the head of his cock where his tongue had just been.

Jake clenched his teeth as the big helmet pressed against his spit-lubricated sphincter. He was certain this was going to hurt, but thought it fair that Ricky should be given the chance to *try* and get it inside him. Mark and Tommy had succumbed to having *his* equally thick and almost as long cock inside *them*, without so much a word of complaint.

99

Ricky began nuzzling the back of Jake's neck again, and wound his long arms about his chest, tweaking his nipples briefly before moving his hands downwards. Wrapping the fingers of his right hand around Jake's hard on, while the fingers of the other tenderly kneaded his balls, he drew back his foreskin the instant he penetrated him, fully and in a single movement. Jake whimpered—not an exclamation of pain, but one of unprecedented pleasure. And the more Ricky moved back and forth, each deep thrust bringing him closer to nirvana, the more he worked his hand up and down his shaft, the more intense this ecstasy became. Jake, who had always been proud of his staying-power, knew this would let him down now. With a loud roar, clenching his sphincter so tight that it almost cut off the other man's blood supply, he blasted his load with such force that it hit the tiles and ricocheted back on to his abs. Seconds later, Ricky gave one last almighty upwards lunge, the power of this raising Jake up on to his tiptoes, and flooded Jake's bowels with a torrent of sperm.

Ricky stayed put, panting, until his cock slackened and slipped out of its own accord.

"My first come in three days," he said, as they dried each other. "Hell, that was *so* powerful, I thought my balls were going to come up as well!"

They got on to the bed, and for a few minutes smoked in silence, Ricky lying in Jake's arms and with his head on his chest, listening to the pounding of his heart.

"So, what happens now?" he asked, after he had put out his cigarette.

"That's up to you, I guess," Jake replied. "What do *you* want to happen?"

Reaching down, Ricky began toying with Jake's damp, flaccid cock—not that he was expecting much to happen, if anything, after the earth-shattering hump in the bathroom.

"What I'm asking is—do you want me to go home?"

Jake kissed the top of Ricky's head, which should have answered his question.

"Do you *want* to go home?" he posed. "*I* don't want you to go home…"

*

They awoke just after nine, having slept in one another's arms on top of the bed. It was Sunday. Outside the window, the sun was shining and the sky cloudless and blue. There was nothing to rush for! Ricky reached down and caressed Jake's heavy, flaccid cock, and it responded at once.

"I want you watch you," he murmured. "I want to watch you getting yourself off."

Jake thought it a strange request. What he really wanted was to flip Ricky over and give him the same servicing as he had received last night in the bathroom. Then he thought about that time in the Storm House, with Mark. Slowly, he began stroking his cock, while Ricky did the same. With Mark, he had *pretended* not to be watching.

"Take your time, baby," Ricky breathed.

The expression on Jake's face was serene as he worked his fleshy foreskin back and forth over the shiny strawberry

101

head of his cock, its slit smiling and damp, with just a hint of pre-cum. Ricky had told him to take his time, yet *he* was almost there, clenching his teeth and edging. Then Jake's cock-head flared like an angry cobra, and his back arched as he spurted three creamy ribbons across his abs. Not letting go of his cock Ricky got up and straddled Jake's thighs, and tossing back his head and shutting his eyes, let rip. Jake counted the spurts—seven of them which criss-crossed his already drenched torso.

"Wow," he panted, flopping on to his back next to Jake. "I needed that…"

Dipping his forefinger into the puddle on Jake's middle, he transferred some of the elixir to his lips.

"Delicious," he purred. "Here—try some."

Jake was reluctant to taste the product of their passion, but did so all the same. It was the first time he had ever tasted sperm—and like Tommy's cock, he was surprised how good it was.

Ten minutes later, they were dressed and breakfasting in the café on the corner of Jake's street.

"So, now what?" Ricky posed when they were finished, and drinking their second cup of coffee. "Do you want to see me again—despite how I earn my crust?"

Jake told him, "That's the daftest thing I ever heard. Of course I do."

Then he began chuckling to himself, and Ricky asked him what was tickling him.

"All this," Jake replied. "Two weeks ago I was milking cows and mucking out pigs. Now I'm taking it up the arse from a Dilly Boy and earning more money than I dreamed of, driving Lord Muck around. Any minute now I'm going to wake up."

Ricky smirked, "Lord Muck? I'd heard out Mr. Stevens was a bit of a tetchy character."

"That's putting it mildly," Jake said. "Lennie seems to hate everybody. But I can handle him."

Ricky had to be somewhere, and got up to leave. He hated shaking hands with the most exciting man he'd had sex with in years, and wanted to snog this stupendous slab of Yorkshire beef, mindless of the other customers in the café. Jake watched him walk away.

"Like as not before he wraps his fingers around my cock again he'll have wrapped them around half a dozen more," he mused to himself. "Yet I don't care. I like him…I like him a lot."

7: Settling Down

July 1964

For Jake, the humble, no-nonsense farmer's boy, life was full of surprises. The last three weeks had zipped by. Not so long ago, his only prospects in life appeared to be endless abuse from his father, and the possibility of heading off to join his brothers in Melbourne. Until recently he had thought himself flagrantly heterosexual. Now he was unsure what he was. Men turned him on, but so did women. Why else would he keep getting a semi each time he saw Lennie Stevens' girlfriend, Martha, and why had he had a wank one night thinking about her? But, he asked himself, if the opportunity arose would he want to have sex with her, or any other female for that matter? Jake guessed he would cross that bridge if he ever came to it, though he doubted that any woman, no matter how voluptuous would compare to what he had experienced since coming to London. He had fucked three men—two to be exact because the third, Ricky, had only fucked *him* thus far in their relationship. Albeit briefly he had sucked a cock, and he had tasted sperm, and enjoyed both! He liked having sex with men, and moreover did not doubt that there would be many more before he embarked on that final journey to the homo harem in the sky.

Jake was chauffeur to a tetchy, prejudiced pop star he did not particularly like, though he was gradually getting used to Lennie because from Day One he had stood up to him, and told him that he found some of his comments very distasteful. Now, Lennie appeared to have stopped making nasty remarks about homosexuals, having seen the effect that Martha was having on Jake, each time they met.

"You fancy her, don't you?" Lennie had asked him, last week when Jake had been driving him to an appointment.

"What man wouldn't?" Jake had responded, truthfully. "But I've always made a point of never going near another bloke's bird."

Then Lennie had shocked him by chirping, "Actually, boyo, I wouldn't mind that at all so long as I was there. We could fuck her together, obviously not at the same time. She talks about us having a threesome all the time."

Jake had almost run the car into the back of a bus at this. Thankfully Lennie had not brought up the subject since.

Jake had not yet told Tommy Vincent about Ricky, but suspected that he must have had an idea that something was going on because, the other day, he had remarked that Jake had gained that spring in his step that only love could bring. Even Lennie had pressed him for answers, wanting to know who the "lucky lady" was.

Last week, Jake had gien Ricky the spare key to the bedsit, to come and go as he pleased, as he was spending more time there than at home, wherever home was. Most evenings, when Jake was driving Lennie around, Ricky turned up at nine, on the dot and with no questions asked by Jake over what he had got up to during his day. *Always* he headed straight for the shower, as if to cleanse himself of his trade. Then they would eat, or sometimes go out if there was not much on television. And *always* they would have hot sex once they hit the sheets, invariably with Ricky in the driving seat. On the rare occasions when Jake was not required by Lennie or Tommy, they went sightseeing.

As for Mark, he had almost been relegated to Jake's past. During his first week in London, Jake had called him every day, and they had talked of a future—of setting up home in Whitby. Since then the calls had been less frequent, though Jake's heart, not to mention his cock, had flipped each time he heard Mark's voice. He was still living at Mill Cottage, but he had put the place up for sale, though so far there had been no prospective buyers. He had seen hide nor hair of Eddie Nelson, and since being shouted to by the landlord of the Cock & Crown had heard no gossip about Jake. Mark had asked Jake, point-blank, if he and Tommy had had sex, and Jake had told him the truth—about the night of passion in the penthouse, of how Tommy had blown him twice in his office, and finally got around to achieving his goal by bending him over his desk. But he had said nothing about Ricky—his lofty, beautiful blond stud who, one night after making love, had whispered in his ear that he loved him.

Tomorrow—Wednesday, 15 July—after three weeks of heaven with Ricky, Jake would be casting himself into the jaws of hell—aka the Tommy Vincent Roadshow, which would see him driving Lennie Stevens up to Liverpool for the first show at the Empire, then up and down the country.

"It's for two weeks, not two years," Ricky told him over breakfast. "I'm still going to be here when you get back, so stop fretting. And we still have tonight…"

Half an hour later, Jake was in Tommy Vincent's office, and Tommy was in a flap. Lennie had disappeared.

"He was supposed to be here first thing," Tommy said. "I've called him, and whoever answered the phone reckons they've no idea where he is. He and Martha went out on the razzle last night, apparently, and they haven't come back."

"Maybe he's got pre-tour nerves," Jake suggested. "Or a hangover."

"He puts bums on seats and sells a lot of records," Tommy told him. "Apart from that, the man's an arsehole. His attitude stinks, and always has. One of these days…"

Jake walked around to Tommy's side of the desk, jerked the drawer open and grabbed the keys for the Rolls-Royce.

"Tell me where he lives and I'll go fetch him," he said. "Maybe he's—"

Tommy cut him short, "That's just it. Nobody seems to *know* where he lives. His bank does but they're not allowed to say. He always asks you to drop him off at the same spot like he did his last driver—he quit because he couldn't cope with Lennie's tantrums. Has he sounded off at you, yet?"

"A couple of times," Jake replied. "When I gave as good as I got, he backed down. He's made a few comments that he'd get a wallop for up in Yorkshire, but I think his bark's worse than his bite. He behaves the way he does because he can't live like the rest of us, walled up in his golden castle."

Tommy whistled through his teeth, "Christ, Jake, where did that come from? Have you ever thought of becoming a psychoanalyst? Lennie hasn't been sucking your cock as well, as he?"

Jake shook his head, "No, but he does want to watch me fucking his girlfriend."

He returned the keys to the drawer, and saw the fiendish look on Tommy's face.

"And—would you do that?" he asked.

Jake shrugged his shoulders, "I'd rather do her than him. But I wouldn't do anybody at all while somebody else was watching. So, what do I do about Lennie? Do I wait here until he shows up?"

"Damn," Tommy exploded, banging his fist on the desk and rattling the phone. "If he doesn't show up, the fucking tour might have to be cancelled. It'll be impossible to find another headliner at such short notice. But there's no point in you hanging around here. Call me, every hour on the hour, while I try work out some sort of contingency plan."

Over the next few hours, Jake covered some distance on foot, and eventually ended up near Hyde Park, where he ate lunch at a pub—washed down by two pints of Guinness. He figured that if Lennie complained of him stinking of ale, it was his fault for messing everyone around.

Outside the park gates was a kiosk, and Jake bought an evening paper, wondering why it was called such when it was only three in the afternoon. Sitting on a wooden bench, his shirt open and with the sun beating down on him, he thanked Fate for bringing him here. Partridge Farm, Eddie Nelson and the women he had known belonged to another world, and could have been a million miles away. Initially he had disliked London, the way everyone rushed around as if their arses were on fire, the traffic noise, the dreadful cost

108

of living. He was not sure how long this new life would last before he threw in the towel and went back North. This depended upon how things worked out with Ricky, buzzing around like a randy bee—here a wank, there a wank, everywhere a wank-wank! Was his lover telling the truth, trying to convince him that this was *all* he ever did for money? Did men really pay him ten-shillings a time just to toss them off? When Ricky breezed into the bedsit on an evening, had he just had his cock inside some smelly old bloke, hence his heading for the shower straight away? Jake was turning this over in his mind when his gaze fell on the headline, on page three of his newspaper:

MAN FOUND STRANGLED IN REGENT'S PARK
FINALLY NAMED.

One of the Dilly Boys, Ricky had told him the other night, adding that his identity was still a mystery. Well, if this was true, Herbert Edwards must have been a "boy" who had come out of retirement to go gobbling off other men in the bushes in the middle of the night! Jake read the piece:

> Herbert Edwards, 71, was a popular figure around Soho. He was found face-down behind a clump of bushes and had been strangled with a school tie. Theft does not appear to have been the motive, as Mr. Edwards was still in possession of his wallet, which is known to have contained a large amount of money. Scotland Yard are still investigating…

Jake chuckled to himself, though it was no laughing matter. A 71-year-old Dilly Boy, with a name like Herbert? Ricky had obviously been mistaken. Yet it was a mistake that had worked in *his* favour—for had Ricky been working that Saturday evening, three weeks ago, wanking of strangers instead of helping out behind the bar in the Golden Lion, the most exciting sex he had *ever* had would never have taken place!

At five o'clock, Jake called Tommy, who told him to get back to the office at once.

"Grab a taxi," he barked. "Sheila will reimburse you when you get here."

Fifteen minutes later, after a harrowing journey which saw the driver zipping through the afternoon rush-hour at break-neck speed, twice mounting the kerb and once almost colliding with a double-decker bus, Jake was in Tommy's office. And there was still no sign of Lennie.

"Where is he?" Jake asked. "You sounded so panicky."

"Liverpool," Tommy growled. "God knows how he got there. Sheila took the call just before you called me. The message was garbled, something to do with Martha. They've had a falling out. You'll have to drive up there in the morning and fetch him back on Friday after the show. Sheila's booked you in at a hotel for a couple of nights."

Sheila gave him instructions. He was to pick up the keys for the Rolls at nine, and drive straight up to Liverpool—a journey of exactly 200 miles. As it was the holiday season, there might be a lot of traffic on the road, therefore it was essential that he didn't make too many stops along the way.

He had been booked into the Regency Hotel, where Lennie was staying, and would drive him to press-conferences, photo-shoots, wherever he wanted to go. Nothing had been decided yet because everything hinged on whatever mood might be in. Jake would also be expected to stand in the wings when Lennie was on stage—not just during the show, but at tomorrow's rehearsals—in case he needed to make a quick getaway from those pesky female fans. Finally—and this the part of Tommy's order sheet that made him titter—he was to get Lennie back to London straight after breakfast on Friday, even if it meant knocking him out and locking him in the boot of the car.

"He sounds like a charmer," Ricky observed, when they met up later for dinner at a little café off Kensington High Street. "Do you think he's on drugs? Most of them are."

Jake told him, "It must be tough, living that kind of life. I mean, I'd never say no to all the money he's earning. But, not being able to step outside your front door without being mobbed? Having to be guarded most of the time? It must tell on the nerves."

Tonight, Ricky looked good enough to eat. It was warm and he was wearing black chinos and a white, short-sleeve shirt, open at the neck to reveal the fan of bristles between his pecs. Ricky felt the same way about Jake, carrying his jacket on account of the heat and whose nipples showed prominently through the thin fabric of his pale-blue T-shirt.

"I'm going to miss you," he said. "I know it's only for a few days, and we've only known each other properly for a few weeks, but I have a good feeling about us."

"Me too," Jake replied, and then, sensing that the mood might turn sombre he asked, "So, how many blokes have you tossed off today?"

Ricky took a sip of his wine, and looked his lover in the eye from over the top of his glass.

"None, and that's the truth," he said. "Since that first night with you I've never stopped thinking about giving it all up and getting a proper job—the sort I trained for. There are so many *ugly* people out there, Jake, and I'm not talking about the way they look. Forget the music business. The sex trade's a tough life, though you mightn't believe me when I say it is. So many of the boys—and girls—end up hooked on something or other, or worse."

"Like Herbert Edwards?" Jake posed. "He was in the paper this afternoon. I guessed he was the one you told me about—the murder in Regent's Park."

"I read that too," Ricky said. "It came as a shock. I knew Herbert—had him as a punter a couple of times. He's a big theatre director from down Charing Cross Road—well, he was. The second time I went with him he paid me three times the going rate to wank into his hanky. Said as how he had an old gas-mask at home, a souvenir of the war, and that he was going to put my hanky inside it and get himself off every night until the smell went away. Sounds yukky, you might think, but if it made him happy, that's all that matters. From what I gather, he also liked them young. The story going around is that the lad's dad saw him sneaking out of the bedroom window late at night—that he followed him and caught them in act, then did poor old Herbert in."

"Ah, the schoolboy tie," Jake put in, wanting to change the subject again. "I wish you could come up to Liverpool with me, but it'd mean you having to travel back by train."

"I promise I'll stay celibate," Ricky told him. "And it won't be sell-a-bit here, sell-a-bit there. Just promise *me* you won't go jumping Lennie's bones while you're away."

After leaving the restaurant, Jake and Ricky took a stroll up Kensington High Street and into Holland Park. There was not much of a moon, not many people around. Jake did not flinch when Ricky reached for his hand—he had never strolled hand-in-hand with anyone in his life, and it felt good, the bolt of electricity which shot through his frame when their fingers interlinked.

"I've been here many times," Ricky said, pointing to a group of tall poplar trees a hundred yards ahead of them. "There's a local legend that says the reason those trees have grown so tall is on account of all the spunk that gets shot under them. If we headed there, we'd be in good company, that's for sure. Don't worry. I'm not going to try perverting you out here under the stars."

They walked back to Jake's place—a fair distance for Ricky, who despite his physique and long legs was not used to extraneous exercise, therefore they stopped off at a pub halfway. Sitting outside sipping their pints, Jake asked him if he had ever had a regular boyfriend.

"I've had affairs that have lasted a couple of months," he said. "As soon as they found out about my extra-curricular activities, they dropped me like a hot spud. You're the first bloke I've ever been upfront with."

"Yet I know nothing about you," Jake told him. "Well, other than you have an enormous knob and that you like tossing off old fellas in backyards and bushes."

"Easy remedied," Ricky smiled, lighting a du Maurier and sliding the pack across the table to Jake. "My name's Richard Ross. East End boy, twenty-seven, six-two, uncut, nine-point-five going on ten, a-hundred-and-sixty pounds, versatile. That's how I'd put if I advertised my wares, which I never have. I live in a little flat off Old Compton Street, left to me by Aunty Doreen. She was the token family lesbian—ran a girls-only gaff in Dean Street. If you came to visit you'd see that it's not a shit-tip, that I have an acquired taste. Anything else, Sherlock?"

Jake reached under the table, gave his knee a squeeze and whispered, "Yes, finish your drink. I'm taking you back to my *gaff*, as you call it, and when we get there I'm going to fuck you all the way into next week and back."

"Music to my ears," Ricky grinned, draining the contents of his glass in one gulp.

The theatres were turning out and the West End bustling with tourists, but once they turned into Jake's street, not a soul was to be seen. Dragging Ricky under a street-lamp, he kissed him—no mere brushing of the lips this time, but a wanton, full-on snog. When he released him, breathless and tingling all over, Ricky started humming "Lili-Marlene"—thinking that Jake would not get the connection.

"It was in the paper," Jake enlightened him. "She's been booked for the Royal Variety Show?"

"Who has?" Ricky wanted to know, grabbing him by the

wrist and leading him to the front entrance. "Come on, big boy. We need to crack on. I've got a big, big load with your name written all over it."

Jake told him, "Marlene Dietrich. It was in the paper. She's booked for the Royal Variety Show. Unless you were just impersonating Tommy Steele. He's on the bill as well."

As usual, Jake was in no hurry to "crack on", though he was intent on teasing his lover a little, prior to the main event. It was warm in the room, and after opening the window he peeled off his T-shirt, kicked off his shoes, and grabbed two bottles of beer from the fridge. Great minds thought alike and Ricky did the same, draping his shirt over the back of his chair. For a few minutes they smoked in silence, sitting opposite each other at the table and staring into one another's eyes, each with his own thoughts.

"Has anybody ever told you how staggeringly lovely you are?" Ricky asked him, at length.

"Many a time, but not in so many words," Jake grinned. "More often than not when I've tanked them up on gin-and-lime and giving them what their husbands can't. Then the next morning when you pass them in the street, pushing their prams and with hubby tagging along, you might just as well be invisible."

"And—don't you find *me* handsome?" Ricky ventured.

Jake shook his head, "Not handsome. Just exquisite. Come on, let's hit the shower. I really do whiff after being out all day in this heat. And no shenanigans in the steam. When I have you for the first time I want it to be on the bed where I can see what I'm doing."

They undressed, Ricky dropping his chinos to reveal that as usual he was wearing nothing underneath—and already sporting an erection so hard that it looked like it might snap off at the roots. He was disappointed that Jake did not even have a semi, even when they started soaping one another up and down under the lukewarm water—or while they were getting dried and Ricky deliberately dropped the towel so that he could stoop to pick it up, and give Jake's cock a little tug and a kiss on the way back up.

They returned to the bedroom and lay facing each other on top of the cotton counterpane, refreshingly cool. Ricky's boner had subsided only slightly, and Jake's cock was still flaccid, hanging heavily over his inner thigh, the head just peeking through the thick, fleshy cowl. Ricky shuddered, a mixture of excitement and apprehension. Every night for three weeks, Jake had taken *his* cock with surprising ease, but he was not sure that he would be able to do the same— though well aware that it was only fair that he should try. Swinging his body around to that they were in sixty-nine position, he took Jake's entire cock into his mouth and it stiffened so quickly and to such an extent that he had to regurgitate it so that he was sucking only the soapy-tasting glans. Jake assumed that Ricky would be expecting him to do the same—that this time, as had happened with Tommy, a peremptory sampling of the goods would not suffice. Opening wide, he took the helmet and a few inches of shaft, and found the taste to his liking, even though Ricky drooled a little precum. However, when he began thrusting too fervently, and he thought he might gag, Jake rolled him onto his back and realised, on account of him being almost two stones heavier, that he was now in complete control. Even so, he wrapped the fingers of one hand around the turgid shaft to be safe. Then *he* got carried away, sucking *so* hard that Ricky stopped gorging and begged him to stop.

"Keep that up and you're going to have me there before the real fun begins," he panted, swinging his body around again so that their profiles were facing on the pillow. "You said you wanted to fuck me…"

"I do," Jake chortled. "But we don't have any stuff."

"Stuff?" Ricky echoed. "You mean lubricant? You don't need lubricant, baby. Just eat me out, like I've eaten you out more times than I care to remember. I haven't had a bloody good rimming in months. Come on, give it a whirl!"

Jake tried not to react. The three men that he'd had sex with had rimmed him, but *he* hadn't asked them to. Yet it had felt so good! He realised he would have to "give it a whirl", but wasn't looking forward to it as Ricky raised his long, hairy legs until his knees touched his nipples. Then, just as he was taking a deep breath and preparing to plunge his face into unchartered territory Ricky giggled, girlishly.

"I was only kidding. If you look in the back pocket of my trousers, you'll find some stuff, as you call it."

Jake got off the bed, and a moment later was unscrewing the cap off the tube while Ricky rolled on to his front and held his breath, not sure he would be capable of taking Jake's log, slightly smaller than his own but gargantuan nevertheless. He also assumed that he would be in for a rough ride from this lusty farmer's boy.

117

Jake may not have relished pushing his tongue inside his lover's hole but he was not averse to giving him a couple of fingers to work him nice and loose. He then wedged his glans against the relaxed ring of muscle and pushed hard— the way Mark and Tommy had liked it—sailing halfway home with his first thrust. Keeping up a steady rhythm, his scrotum slapping against Ricky's tailbone like wet leather, he brought him to heights even he had rarely experienced before withdrawing completely, not wanting to explode just yet. Kneeling back, he glanced down at the gaping, winking chasm and for a moment *was* tempted to go down on it, and would have done had it not been for the lubricating cream.

"Ready for the finale?" he purred.

Ricky groaned his approval as Jake dug his fists under his sticky pits and brought him up on to his knees. This time he penetrated him slowly, but as soon as he started fucking again he was no longer Jake Nelson, farm boy, but a wild, rampant stallion. Sweat streaked down Ricky's back as he pressed the flats of his hands against the wall for support, trickling down his spine, between his cheeks and into his crack, offering Jake extra lubrication. Cupping one pec in each hand he stabbed upwards, while Ricky whimpered like an injured puppy. He had assumed rightly—Jake *was* rough, but it was a *beautiful* roughness which he wanted to go on for ever, even though his thighs had started to cramp. Then Jake dropped his hands—one to massage Ricky's balls, rolling them around in their now-tightening sack, the other to wrap itself around his cock to begin bringing him off. As Jake was getting close,

118

he slowed down until he was hardly moving at all. And just as he gave a loud groan and flooded Ricky's insides with his hot, copious load, Ricky screwed his eyes shut and blasted half a dozen streamers across the headboard.

The next morning, there was barely time to say goodbye. Through bleary eyes, Jake glanced at his watch. It was twenty-to-nine, and they had overlaid. Jumping out of bed, he rushed into the bathroom and took a quick shower. When he returned Ricky was wide awake, spread-eagled on top of the counterpane, toying with his hard-on, the woebegone expression on his face like that of a child who has just been told that Santa Claus does not exist.

"Don't tell me this has to go to waste?" he moaned.

Jake dressed quickly, cursing time and its tyranny. Then, sitting on the edge of the mattress, he wrapped his fingers around Ricky's cock, and brought him off in two minutes flat. Ricky arched his back, spraying his load everywhere and drenching Jake's fist. Stooping over him, Jake kissed him. Then, quite unexpectedly, he went down on his cock and sucked him hard, swallowing the final salty-sweet remnants of his load before standing up and licking his fingers clean.

"Just make sure you lock the door when you go out," he told him. "I'll be back Friday afternoon. If you're not here, leave a note saying where we can meet up."

He kissed him, grabbed his suitcase from the top of the wardrobe, and left. Ricky did not observe that his eyes had welled with tears.

8: Liverpool

July 1964

It was five-minutes after nine when Jake reached Tommy Vincent's office. Tommy was not in, and Sheila passed him the car-keys through the hatch, along with an envelope.

"Money for expenses," she told him. "The hotel room's paid for. Have a nice trip. Don't do anything I wouldn't."

He chuckled at this, and headed for the stairs.

The drive up to Liverpool was long, but uneventful. He stopped off for lunch at a roadside service station, took his time eating it, and had a half-hour nap in the car park to refresh himself before resuming his journey. It amused him when the couple who had parked next to him observed the car and obviously mistook him for someone important, and took a picture. It was after five when he drew up in front of the Regency Hotel. A tuxedoed majordomo relieved him of the car keys, and a bellboy took his suitcase and showed him up to his room—sticking out his hand for a tip. Jake had never tipped anyone before, and assumed that a shilling would be sufficient, until the young man's expression told him otherwise and he gave him another.

The room was huge, the bed big enough to accommodate four men his size—and what he initially thought was a safe, in one corner, was a well-stocked drinks cabinet. Inside the wardrobe was a real safe, and a trouser-press. The bathroom was in proportion to everything else. Jake had never seen a circular tub before, and with what looked like gold-plated fixtures on it and the shower and washbasin. Above this was a shelf lined with toiletries. He had uncapped a bottle and was sniffing the contents when there was a tap on the door. It was Lennie Stevens, and he was wearing a black silk dressing-gown, and at this time of the day! Shouldering past Jake, he walked into the room.

"How was the drive up here?" he asked, flatly.

"Okay," Jake replied, wondering whether he should ask Lennie why he had not waited to come up here in the Rolls, instead of suddenly disappearing and leading everyone a merry dance. "How was the rehearsal?"

"Bloody awful, boyo" he growled. "I have a really bad feeling about tonight. Why Tommy had to start the tour in Liverpool baffles me. They're not interested in foreigners up here, as they label anybody that comes from London. Well, you're not London, but you know what I mean. I was talking to one of the promoters earlier, and he reckons this Mersey-sound thing is here to stay."

Jake went to the cabinet and poured himself a beer, then poured one for his unexpected guest. He had heard Tommy Vincent grumbling about the same thing—the fact that the pop charts were choc-a-bloc with singers and groups from Liverpool, but that he was confident that Lennie's career was so secure, not even the best of these would knock him off his self-important pedestal.

"I don't know much about this stuff," he said. "Maybe it's a flash in the pan, like Lonnie Donegan and skiffle."

Lennie slumped into a chair. His dressing-gown was open, displaying an expanse of light-brown chest hair—and when he splayed his legs wide he showed more than enough of his hairy inner thighs to make Jake feel more than a little uncomfortable. He wondered what the singer's fans would say—not to mention Lennie himself—if they knew that one of Britain's premier entertainers was sitting half-dressed in the bedroom of a man who, though a late developer, liked having sex with other men.

"If you'd have been at the rehearsal, you'd have seen for yourself," Lennie told him. "I *felt* like a foreigner with all that Liverpool twang going on around me. They all seem to talk down their noses. Tony Milano's on the bill, and he's the only one I could understand. Martha used to be his bird until she found out he batted for the other team. That's one of the perks of this business, women flinging themselves at you all the time because you're in the limelight. How many women have *you* fucked, Jake?"

It was a pretty direct if not impertinent question, though Jake saw no reason to lie.

"Twenty or so," he replied. "I never counted them."

"Twenty," the other posed. "And how old are you, Jake? Twenty-five?"

"Twenty-one," he lied. "I got the key to the door last November…!

"Twenty birds," Lennie exclaimed. "That's an awful lot of pussy for a bloke as young as you, more than I'd had when I was your age. But I'm happy about that. It makes me feel more comfortable in your company."

Jake pretended to be offended, "Why *more* comfortable? Did you think there was summat wrong with me before?"

Lennie chuckled, "And now I've insulted you. I meant Tommy. He never hires anybody unless he thinks there's a chance of them dropping their pants. That never happened with me. We weren't put on this earth to shove our cocks up one another's arseholes. My old man used to say that Hitler had the right idea when it came to dealing with queers, and since coming into this business I'm starting to think he was right. This business is full of them."

He glanced at his watch, and finished his drink. Jake had not minded Lennie *thinking* he was homosexual. He was however *deeply* offended by the suggestion that homosexuals needed to be put to death in concentration camps. If he had deliberated between liking and not liking Lennie before, that one comment from the singer had gone a long way towards helping him make up his mind.

Lennie got up, squeezed his shoulder and said, "I'll see you in the restaurant. Shall we say nine? There's bugger all else to do in this town. I think I'll be having an early night. Martha's minge will appreciate that!"

*

Jake was not sure what he should be wearing for dinner in a five-star hotel. He had not packed a tie, and had not brought a suit with him from Yorkshire. It was a warm evening. He therefore told himself if the restaurant didn't like the way he was dressed in his short-sleeved shirt and slacks he would eat at the Wimpy Bar he had passed on his way here. Whatever, he was not looking to sharing a table with Lennie after his latest comments about homosexuals.

He went downstairs at ten-minutes to nine, and as there was no sign of Lennie he went to the restaurant bar and ordered a pint of beer. The bar was empty save for a lanky, fair-haired man sitting at the counter. The man—he was in his mid-twenties and hardly looked inconspicuous in a vivid pink shirt and skin-tight turquoise trousers—had the most enormous quiff and was drinking Guinness. He introduced himself as Alan, and spoke with a Liverpool accent. He also had a slight stammer.

"I've seen you around," he pronounced. "Aren't you Lennie Stevens' driver?"

Jake nodded, took the stool next to his, and asked Alan if he knew Lennie.

"Sort of," he replied. "Does that mean you also work for Tommy Vincent?"

Jake nodded again, and asked Alan if he knew him, too.

"Everybody in the business knows Tommy Vincent," he said, his lean face breaking into a wide grin. "Some of us only too well, mate. Has he tried it on with you yet?"

Jake was about to ask what he meant by this—though he knew exactly what he meant, and was merely curious at what Alan's response would be—when Lennie entered the restaurant. The look he gave Alan was one of pure poison. Finishing his drink, he shook hands with the Liverpudlian.

"Very nice meeting you, Jake," Alan told him. "Just be careful while you're walking through Tommy Vincent's rose-garden. There's an awful lot of pricks about."

Jake took his place at the table opposite Lennie—and the

glare he gave him could have soured milk. As if expecting trouble, Alan made a hasty exit, leaving his drink.

"Do you *know* who that is?" Lennie asked, then without waiting for an answer added, "You told me you weren't a queer. So why were you talking to Rory Storm? He's as bent as a nine-bob note. You only have to look at what he's wearing. Twenty-five and still living with his mother. If that isn't a giveaway that he's the biggest sissy since Liberace, I don't know what is."

Jake smiled, though all he really wanted to do was punch Lennie in the face.

"Where I come from, lots of twenty-five-year-olds live with their mothers," he said. "That doesn't make them what you say they are. He told me his name was Alan—"

"Alan Caldwell," Lennie shot back. "That's his real name, but we all know him as Rory Storm, the moniker given him by his manager who's even more bent than he is. Rumour has it he beds his discoveries the same as Tommy does, then gives them monikers judging on how they fared in bed. Billy Fury was furious under the bedsheets, Johnny Quick suffered from premature ejaculation, and Rory Storm makes a lot of noise when he's shooting his muck. He once offered to take me under his wing. Wanted to call me Lennie Load…"

This made Jake laugh out loud.

"Lennie Load. I like that!"

Lennie elaborated, "Some of these managers are really seedy, Jake. You already know what Tommy's like. I'm not the only one who turned him down. Rory Storm's manager is an arsehole. He gets them to drop their trousers even if they're disgusted with that. They want money and fame. Then the manager threatens them with exposure to the press if they don't toe the line and *keep* dropping their trousers. I'd line the lot of them up against a wall and put a bullet through their skulls. He didn't touch *you*, did he or make any improper suggestions? You'd be well within your rights to give him a pasting, if he did."

Jake sighed, "Lennie, I like my job and I like driving you around, and maybe it's not my place to say this—but I think you should start being nice to people. A lot of folk out there really like you, but I don't think they'd like you any more if they heard some of the things you said."

Lennie held up one hand, as if warding off a blow.

"I'm sorry," he said. "You're right, I do behave like a twat, sometimes. That's what this business does to you. Friends, eh?"

They shook hands, and as his was caught in a grip of steel, the singer shuddered as if afraid of the younger man. Throughout the meal—the cost of which, Jake estimated, would have fed him and his father for a week back home— their conversation was restrained, steering well clear of "queers", shonky managers, and show business in general. Jake told Lennie about life on the farm, of how he would have done anything short of killing him to get away from Eddie Nelson. Lennie spoke of his pre-fame life in Bow, where he said only true Cockneys came from, and this made Jake think about Ricky and wonder what he might have been getting up to.   Lennie confided in Jake about his

126

troubled childhood, raised by a single mother who had died ten years ago—the day after his nineteenth birthday. But when Jake asked him about his living arrangements, why he always wanted to be dropped off at a certain spot, instead of allowing Jake to drive him all the way home, Lennie was reluctant to make him any the wiser.

The show, the following evening, was an eye-opener for Jake, who until now had only ever seen these famous faces on the television, or staring back at him from the pages of music magazines. He could not help wondering what lay beneath the surface of some of these stars—if any of them were as horrid, away from the limelight, as Lennie Stevens.

Tommy Vincent had stipulated that Jake remain in the wings throughout the entire show: five acts each performing four songs, and Lennie ending the show with six, more if the crowd called for an encore. Billy J Kramer he found to be polite, Freddie Garrity & The Dreamers likewise but daft with their on-stage gyrations. Gerry & The Pacemakers he found maudlin, though the audience screamed the place down before joining in with "You'll Never Walk Alone". He liked Brian Poole and the Tremeloes, but the act that got to him most of all was Rory Storm & The Hurricanes.

Vocally, Rory—or Alan, as he had introduced himself— was flat as the proverbial fart, and the way he kept rolling his eyes around suggested he might have partaken of something before his performance. In his powder blue suit, and with his huge blond quiff sprinkled with glitter dust, he came across as more than slightly effeminate, but there was something about him that Jake found appealing and which reminded him of Ricky—so much so that, halfway through Rory's set, he found himself pushing his hands inside his trousers to straighten out his developing hard-on.

When Lennie Stevens walked on to the stage while the cheers for the Liverpudlian were still rocking the Empire he was greeted with a storm of boos, which grew only louder as he progressed through his opening song. He was a few bars into his second number when a man's shoe whizzed past his ear—this hit the drummer, positioned a few yards behind him, and the boos turned to guffaws of laughter.

Lennie glanced at Jake, as if to say, "Any second now, boyo, and I'm out of here!"

Jake reminded himself how unpleasant Lennie had been to homosexuals and women. And now, *he* was suffering prejudice from this hostile crowd, and for no other reason that he was the only non-Liverpudlian act on the bill.

"Piss off back to London, you poncy Cockney bleeder!" someone yelled from the front row.

Unable to help himself, and deciding that two wrongs did not necessarily make a right, Jake marched on to the stage. Even Lennie seemed surprised. Two security men, standing in the wings, assumed that this was the singer's bodyguard, coming on to lead him off, and stayed put. Then Jake grabbed the mike out of Lennie's hand.

"Listen here, you lot," he bawled, temporarily blinded by the spotlight. "Lennie's come all the way up here to sing to you, not to be insulted. How would you lot like it of the boot was on the other foot? Give him a chance—please!"

128

The audience grew quiet as Jake handed the mike back to Lennie, and the band struck up the introduction to "Let Me Be The Man Of Your Dreams", the song Jake had witnessed—and suffered—him recording in the studio. He returned to the wings, and a moment later felt a movement behind him. It was Rory Storm.

"That took guts," he said in Jake's ear. "I think it's the Northern accent that did it. Always be proud of the fact that you don't pronounce your aitches. I don't like Lennie one bit, and I don't buy all that womanising shit for one second, but there was no need for them to behave like that. Tell me, Jake—what are you doing after the show?"

"Going back to my room," he responded. "Why?"

Pressing his lips closer to Jake's ear, Rory breathed, "Do you feel like having a drink—and maybe a little fun? Know what I mean?"

Jake knew exactly what he meant, and so did his cock. He nodded. After all, what did he have to lose by adding a singer to his roster of lovers?

"I'm on the second floor of the hotel," Rory said. "Room Twenty-Three…"

Jake turned around to say something but the lofty singer was gone. Meanwhile, Lennie's new song brought such a reaction from the audience—whoops and cheers this time—that he had to sing it again. He walked off the stage to a huge applause, his face dripping with sweat, and shook Jake warmly by the hand.

"I owe you one, mate," he said. "Give me a little while to freshen up, and I'll see you in your room."

Twenty minutes later, Jake was back at the hotel. He had showered, and was deliberating between heading for Rory's room, or waiting for Lennie, with whom did *not* want to have a little fun, if this was what he had meant by telling him he "owed him one". He thought of what Rory had said, his suggestion that Lennie's womanising may have been a cover for his true sexual leanings.

"If he wasn't such a turd, I'd have him like lightning," he thought to himself. "*If* he's that way inclined, that is…."

He had lit a cigarette and was still deliberating what to do when there was a tap on the door. It was Lennie, wearing the same black silk dressing-gown as before. His hair was damp, and he brought into the room with him a pungent whiff of expensive cologne. Also as before, he strode across to the drinks cabinet, helped himself to a miniature whisky, and flopped into a chair.

"Thank God that's over with," he groaned. "Talk about pulling teeth. You did good, Jake. I appreciate that…"

Jake smiled and said, "So why do I somehow get the impression there's a 'but' coming?"

Lennie took a swig of whisky, and it took his breath.

"Rory Storm," he said. "You were chatting him up last night at the bar. Tonight he was all over you like a bloody rash. Is there something you're not telling me, Jake? Are you queering him, boyo?"

Jake had not heard the word used as a verb before. He decided he didn't need this any more—or the job.

"I wasn't chatting anybody up," he levelled. "Alan—or Rory, whatever—just happened to be there. If you ask me,

130

you've got homosexuals on the brain, and you obviously don't like women very much. Is there summat *you're* not telling *me*, Lennie—such as every time you come into my room, you're always half-dressed. Sorry to disappoint you, *boyo*, but you're really not my type."

The Lennie's smug expression dropped like a stone, not sure if Jake was being serious, or just kidding. He decided to inject a little humour into the proceedings.

"So, if I came over there and kissed you—what would happen then?"

"I suppose you'd only find that out if you tried," Jake retorted, looking him in the eye.

Unintentionally or not he had clenched his fist and when Lennie observed the size of this, and not for the first time envisaged the damage it might cause, he opted to end the charade.

"I had to know," he said. "For Martha's sake…"

"And I want to be left alone," Jake snapped back. "Why don't you toddle along and give Tommy a call so's he can give me my marching orders for standing up to the mighty Lennie Sevens? And what has *any* of this got to do with Martha?"

At this, Lennie burst out laughing.

"Nobody's going to give you your marching orders, you daft sod," he cracked. "I really did appreciate you walking out on to that stage tonight. I was only kidding about the fairy stuff. I know you're no more of a bloody homo than I am. Which is why I got to thinking. You've watched one of my performances. How's about I watch one of yours?"

131

Jake shot him a puzzled glance.

"What do you mean, one of my performances?"

Lennie gave it to him straight, "Jake—I want to watch you fucking my girlfriend."

Jake's eyes opened wide. Forgetting his beer, he grabbed a miniature from the cabinet. Unscrewing the cap with his teeth, he downed the contents in one gulp.

"And why would you want to do that?" he asked.

Lennie helped himself to one of Jake's cigarettes.

"Because it's what I like to do every now and then," he said. "We're in what's called an open relationship. I like to watch other blokes opening her up, especially after a night like tonight when I'm too knackered to open her up myself. Do you have a problem with that, Jake? Not up to it?"

"Very funny," Jake quipped. "What does Martha have to say about all this?"

Lenny told him, "Martha's been gagging for you ever since that day in the studio. She's waiting for you in my room, naked as a jaybird and wet as October. Don't tell me you're shy about another bloke watching you tomming his bird? Or were you telling porkies when you said you'd had all those women? The way I see it, you're either a virgin or you really *are* a homo. Time to prove yourself, son!"

Jake realised that as long as he was working for Tommy Vincent and driving this odious man around—he assumed not for much longer—Lennie would never stop taunting or questioning him about his sexuality. Also, the last thing he wanted was for this gob-shite to start spreading rumours about him, even if they *did* happen to be true.

132

"Fine," he said, grabbing another miniature to take with him, for Dutch courage. "Let's get on with it."

Lennie's suite was a tip: clothes scattered everywhere, nylon stockings hanging from the curtain rail, an ashtray tipped on to the carpet and the mess not cleaned up, and empty bottles that had just been thrown on to the floor. Martha was sitting cross-legged on the bed, stark naked. Jake caught his breath, not quite expecting this! He realised that he was prostituting himself without actually getting paid—that he was allowing himself effectively to be blackmailed, to prove to Lennie that he was what the singer considered normal.

It was a feeling of *déja vu* as Martha giggled, and tossed back her long blonde hair.

"Hello, big boy," she purred. "Tell me, Jake—are you big all over?"

"I recall you asking me that once before," he reacted.

Then Lennie barked, "The bathroom's over there, if you want to prepare yourself..."

Jake was still not sure that this was a good idea. While in the bathroom he thought about Rory—on the face of it the better bet for tonight, despite Martha's beauty and hourglass figure. He wondered whether he should strip naked here, or if doing so in the bedroom would constitute a part of his performance as Lennie called it. He opted for the former, and sprayed cologne under his arms. Then he changed his mind and put his briefs back on. Lennie had pulled up an armchair and was sitting next to the bed. Martha was now spread-eagled in the middle of it—like a sacrificial virgin on the altar, though Jake didn't doubt that this virgin had been on the altar more than a few times.

"Wow, you *are* a big boy," she piped, sounding like a heroine in a quota-quickie movie. "What muscles you have. You must spend all of your spare time in the gym!"

Jake told her, "I've never been to a gym in my life. I do—did—all my working out with weights in the barn."

"Ah, yes," she purred. "Lennie told me you were a farm boy. Does that mean that you're hung like a stud bull?"

To which Lennie chimed in, "You're gonna find that out soon enough, babe!"

And Jake was thinking to himself, "What the bloody hell *have* I got myself into here, with these two?"

He thought about Rory, wondering what *he* would look like naked with his long legs splayed wide. Then he blinked himself back to reality. He had gone too far to turn back, and approached the foot of the bed. There was no denying Martha was more attractive than any female he had been with in Brodsworthy. Shapely legs, bulbous breasts and narrow waist, and a trimmed pussy which, though he had not seen one in while, caused his balls to flip in their pouch.

"I can see you like me, Jake," she murmured. "Do you like my tight little cunt, as well?"

"It's lovely," he responded, not sure that he liked to hear such a word coming out of a woman's mouth. "Shouldn't I be using protection, though?"

Quick as a flash, Lennie tossed him a packet of Durex. Then Jake dropped his briefs, and there was a sharp intake of breath from the other two.

"Fuck me," Lennie muttered. "He *is* hung like a bull…"

Jake opted for a little malevolent humour of his own.

"Actually, Lennie, I'm *not* going to fuck you, but I guess I could make an exception if you asked me nicely."

The blank expression on Lennie's face suggested that he may have taken this seriously.

"And I don't want *that* inside me," Martha protested. "I mean the rubber thingy. I'm on the bloody pill!"

On cue, Lennie grabbed her bag from the top bedside cabinet, dipped inside it, and showed Jake the packet.

"Using a johnny is like eating with a garden fork," he observed. "And on the subject of eating, how's about seeing some action?"

Climbing on to the bed, Jake raised Martha's legs until her feet were hooked over his shoulders, then plunged his face into her pussy. He had rarely done this with his other women, and was not sure that he was doing it properly —until Martha screamed as if she had been scalded.

"Oh, Jake," she yelled. "It's not your tongue that I want, it's that huge baby's arm with an apple on the end!"

Moving upwards, Jake slid his helmet inside her. He didn't want to kiss her, but did so if only to stop her from making so much noise. It felt good, penetrating a woman after so long, but he still wished that it could have been Rory. For several minutes he moved slowly, not sure why he couldn't get all of his cock inside her—whether it was because she was so tight, as she had boasted, or because he was bigger than she was used to. Withdrawing, he went down on her again, and slurped around and tasted where his

135

cock had been, and this got her really wet. Thankfully she had stopped yelling. Then he pushed his cock back inside her, and this time she took all nine inches.

"That feels *so* good," Martha moaned.

"Likewise," Jake breathed, and meant it.

Then he looked up and saw that Lennie had opened his dressing-gown, to start stroking his cock. At first, Jake averted his gaze—then suddenly he didn't give a damn.

"Does it give you a kick—watching me wanking myself off?" the singer asked him.

Jake chuckled, "Not particularly. But don't stop on my account…"

He was thinking about Lennie's boast—of how he was getting so much of the real thing that he had not had a wank in three years. As a person he found Lennie repulsive. As an object of desire, he had an amazing body—a spectacularly hairy chest, and an attractive uncut cock, albeit on the small side, which probably explained why *he* was making Martha feel good, right now.

Lying further back in the chair, Lennie spread his thighs wide and closed his eyes. Then he started moaning, as his furry abs tightened.

"Don't do it yet, Lennie," Jake rapped. "I'm not ready to fetch just yet. Slow down—and open your eyes. You said you wanted to watch, and we're coming to the best bit!"

Withdrawing his cock. Jake encouraged Martha to get on all fours, that much closer to Lennie so that he was afforded a perfect view of the action. Slamming back into Martha, he made her squeal like a stuck pig, and for fifteen minutes rutted like his life depended on it. Then he slowed down, aware that his climax was imminent.

"Come on, Lennie," he panted. "Whack that knob. Let's both fetch together…"

And Martha was whimpering, "Do that, Lennie. Blast that big fucking load just for me!"

Lennie let out a roar and exploded three ribbons across his chest and abs. Jake grinned. Unable to hold back any longer, he whipped his cock out of Martha and, standing on the mattress aimed his cock at Lennie just as his balls started to churn. Lennie had finished ejaculating and closed his eyes once more, just as Jake blew a massive load across his face. Lennie started to gag, but did not throw up.

"Dirty bastard," he spat. "You just came in my mouth!"

Jake chuckled, climbed off the bed, grabbed Lenny by the hair and, forcing his head back, kissed him passionately on the mouth.

"Well, Lenny—you *are* a cunt," he purred. "Oh, and you can find yourself another driver. I'm sick of hearing you insulting people. I'm off back to London on the train."

His cock still hard and drooling, Jake put on his briefs. Then he went into the bathroom and quickly dressed. When he returned to the bedroom, Martha was lying on the bed, still traumatised after her orgasm, and Lenny had grabbed a handful of tissues and was wiping the sperm off his face. Reaching down, Jake gave his cock a tug.

"The only nice thing about you," he mused.

Two minutes later, he was standing outside the door of Room 23.

9: Scandal!

July 1964

After packing his suitcase, Jake called Mark from the phone in his room. Later he would ask himself *why* he had called Mark, and not Ricky. In any case, there was no reply, so he called Tommy Vincent.

"I've had it with Lennie-bloody-Stevens," he told him. "I'm sorry, Tommy, but I'm handing the car keys to the majordomo, or whatever he's called, and I'm coming back on the train. If you want to sack me, I'm okay with that."

Tommy chortled at the other end of the line, "No need for that, old son. Drive the car back here, and let *him* travel back on the train. Oh, and I've no intention of sacking you, so you can stick *that* in your pipe and smoke it!"

Jake chose not to breakfast in the hotel—the last person he wanted to bump into was Lennie—so he ate at a café in the next street. It was just after five in the when he parked the Rolls in Tommy Vincent's garage, but instead of going up to the office he headed for the bedsit on the off-chance that Ricky would be there. He wasn't. A note left on the kitchen table, on top of which Ricky had placed his key, announced that he had gone to visit an aunt in Brighton, but that he would be back tomorrow. Jake was disappointed. At one stage during the drive down from Liverpool he had become so horny, thinking about Ricky—and his brief encounter with Rory Storm—that he had thought on pulling into a lay-by and having a wank. Then he had changed his mind—better to save it, and put it better use, later! Now, he was tired. There was a chicken pie in the freezer. He shoved this in the oven while he was showering, and ate it while watching a documentary on the television. By eleven he was in bed, fast asleep.

The next morning he awoke refreshed—a slight touch of backache on account of the excessive driving, but ready to face the new day. Rather than cook breakfast—there was hardly anything left in the fridge and he didn't want to eat frozen again—he ate at the café on the corner of the street. He then spent an hour shopping for groceries, and took his purchases back to the bedsit. He was about to leave when the phone rang. It was Tommy.

"Jake, you'd better get your arse around here," he barked and then hung up.

Jake set off. Yesterday, Tommy had promised his job would be safe. He now assumed that Lennie would have been in touch, and that Tommy would have changed his mind. When he arrived at the office, the place was deserted. Tommy was manning the reception desk.

"Where is everybody?" Jake asked. "Where's the fire?"

He followed Tommy into his office, expecting some sort of showdown and not really giving two hoots. London had provided him with an interesting, extended if not expensive holiday for which he had been handsomely remunerated. So far he had not touched the money in his bank account. And as all good things must come to an end…

"I'm not going to apologise, if that's what you're hoping for," he told Tommy. "Lennie's been a pain in the arse since the day I met him. He got what was coming to him."

139

Tommy wore a worried frown.

"You *hit* him?" he asked. "He didn't say anything about *that* when he called."

"Then what *did* he say?" Jake wanted to know.

Tommy enlightened him, "He says he went to your room to borrow your lighter because he'd lost his…that he caught you doing the horizontal foxtrot with his girlfriend."

Jake laughed, and explained what had really happened.

"*That* I would have paid good money to see," Tommy said. "Lennie Stevens and his face covered in spunk. And you snogged him as well!"

"So why *have* you asked me here, if not to sack me?" Jake pressed. "What's the urgency? Where is everybody?"

"One of the girls is getting married, so I gave them all the day off," Tommy replied. "There's just you and me. And I have to tell you, Jake, my arse is *very* hungry. I just gave it a good wash and it almost bit my hand off."

"In that case, the best thing to do is feed it," Jake smiled, unbuckling his belt.

Backing Tommy up against the door, Jake dropped the latch to make doubly sure they would not be disturbed. He recalled last time, how Tommy had done all the work. Now it was his turn. His last sex had been with a woman, and it had felt good spending time inside a wet pussy, even if his performance had been monitored by her odious boyfriend. Now, he needed a man. Undoing Tommy's trousers, he pulled these and his boxers down to his ankles. Tommy's cock, hard and ready for action, poked out from under the hem of his shirt. Tommy shut his eyes as their lips effected a head-on collision, and moment later Jake slid his log under Tommy's balls and began rocking back and forth, copulating with his perineum.

"I want it inside me," Tommy murmured. "*Deep* inside me. Fuck me, Jake. Fuck me like you hate the whole world and its mother!"

Sinking to his knees, and reminding himself that he was getting more adventurous with every passing day, Jake held Tommy's rigid cock upright so that he could lick under his nutty-flavoured scrotum, bouncing his gonads off the flat of his tongue. Then he traced a spittle-line all the way up his spunk-pipe, and ran the edge of his tongue several times around the coronal ridge before taking the glans into his mouth. Tommy made a little whimpering sound and drooled a liberal quantity of precum. Jake ploughed down on the shaft, for the very first time taking a man to the back of his throat, burying the tip of his nose into Tommy's neatly-trimmed pubes, and sucked so hard on him that after just a few minutes Tommy begged him to stop.

"Careful, baby, or you'll have me blowing the lot…"

Jake's cock was so stiff that the strawberry head was pressed against his fluffy abs. Grabbing hold of Tommy's tie, he led him across the room towards his desk. Tommy had obviously planned this when calling him—the tube of lubrication was in the stationary tray, next to the phone, and Tommy made a grab for this.

"We won't be needing that," Jake drawled, forcing him over the arm of the leather chair.

Tommy had asked for it rough and Jake had no intention

141

of disappointing the boss. Squatting on his haunches, his cock popping a rare crystal bubble, he thumbed the older man's cheeks apart.

He was thinking to himself, "I ate pussy properly for the first time last night, so I'm sure I can do this…"

The other night, Jake had eaten a man out for the first time and enjoyed the experience, even though this part of Ricky's anatomy *had* been incredibly hairy. Tommy's was smooth as an egg, making his purple sphincter appear more pronounced as Jake aimed the point of his tongue against the hole. Like Tommy's leaky cock, this tasted good! *So* good, in fact, that he could not get enough of it—slobbering and slurping around the hard ring of muscle, opening it up so that he could explore the interior, which he found tasted even better! After a little while, once he stopped troughing, he found that he could get one, two and then *three* fingers inside, causing Tommy to groan so loudly as to make him relieved there was no one on the other side of the door.

Standing up, he wedged his cock between Tommy's soggy cheeks, and slid inside him with no effort at all. He started the fuck slowly, rocking back and forth on the balls of his feet while Tommy rotated his hips and pushed back on to him—as if nine inches were insufficient to satisfy his lust. And all the while, his cut cock dripped like a tap on to the seat of the chair. Winding one arm about Tommy's waist, Jake dug his fingertips into his pubes—afraid of touching Tommy's cock in case he exploded before *he* wanted him to. Then, he realised that the "iffiness" of the location had got him too excited, that he would probably be

142

incapable of hanging on for much longer. His palm saturated with Tommy's precum, he worked it up and down the rock-hard shaft and Tommy let out a lengthy sigh as he sprayed his load across the seat of the chair. Seconds later, Jake bent his knees and began thrusting upwards, lifting Tommy inches off the carpet as he blasted his juice deep inside his bowels.

For a moment, they remained still. Then Jake decided that he wanted to be *really* daring on what he still regarded his ongoing journey of discovery. Thinking of how he had pulled out of Martha to taste where his cock had been, he withdrew slowly and getting down in his haunches plunged his face into Tommy's crack and sucked hard, gorging on his warm, just-shot load. His hard-on had not subsided, and he was confident he would be capable of doing Tommy again. Then, as he was about to push his cock back inside him, the bell rang at the front desk—three times. Quickly, they pulled up their clothes, and—tossing Jake a box of tissues to mop up the mess on the chair—Tommy went into the outer office to see what all the fuss was about.

"I'm coming," he yelled. "Keep your hair on!"

"You already have," Jake chuckled to himself, tossing the tissues into the bin. "Half a gallon, by the looks of it…"

Two men were standing at the reception hatch. One was middle-aged, plump and balding. The other was tall, in his early twenties. They flashed their badges.

"DS Keith Morris," the older man announced. "This is my colleague, DC Damien Fellows. Would you mind if we came in?"

Tommy showed them into his office, where Jake was perched on the edge of the desk wearing an innocent expression. The officers showed their badges once more.

"So, what's all this about?" Tommy asked.

DS Morris held up a photograph of Lennie Stevens.

"Do you know this man, sir?"

Tommy nodded, "I should imagine everybody knows him. I'm his manager. What's he done this time?"

DC Fellows addressed Jake, "And you, sir? What was your relationship with Mr. Stevens?"

"I'm his driver," Jake replied. "Well, he likes to call me his chauffeur."

"And when did you last see him?" DC Fellows enquired.

Jake told him, "The night before last, in Liverpool. He was appearing in a show there—"

"You had a row with him and left in a huff," DS Morris put in. "What were you arguing about, Mr. Nelson?"

"We weren't," Jake began. "He said—"

"I beg to differ," the detective argued. "Mr. Stevens' girlfriend claims that you gave him quite a mouthful before storming off into the night."

"Well, in a manner of speaking," Jake responded, half to himself. "What's all this about?"

For now, neither of the officers was saying.

"Mr. Nelson," DC Fellows posed. "Were you having a relationship with Martha Longhurst?"

At this, Jake burst out laughing.

"You're taking the mick," he said. "Martha Longhurst? Isn't she the old busybody in *Coronation Street*?"

The older detective saw the funny side of this. Then his expression dropped like a stone.

"Gentlemen," he pronounced. "Mr. Steven's body was found yesterday afternoon in the basement of the Regency Hotel. Initial reports suggest that he'd hung himself."

*

Lennie's death was announced on the lunchtime news. The first report stated that it was being treated as suspicious, and added that as yet the police had given no additional details. This did not prevent the early evening papers from drawing the obvious conclusions—that drugs might been involved. Martha Longhurst was still in Liverpool, being comforted by her parents.

Tommy Vincent accompanied the detectives to the local station. Jake was told he would be questioned later, though it had already been ascertained that he could not have been involved in the tragedy. The hotel receptionist had seen him leaving, and half an hour later when Lennie had come down to breakfast he had seemed in an affable mood. Obviously, something had happened between then and 3.25 pm. when the maid had found him after sneaking down to the cellar for a crafty cigarette.

Jake returned to the bedsit, baffled by all of this. He was not *pleased* that Lennie was dead, but neither could he be a hypocrite and feel sad because the man had been so vile. All he could think about was those last few moments in Lennie's room—how he had exacted his revenge by giving

145

him a face full of cum, *and* a sloppy kiss before grabbing his cock. It was ironic that the last person who had touched this had been one of the homosexuals he so loathed.

Jake knew that if Lennie had not been a wealthy pop star he might have thumped him for some of the comments he had made. But in the brief time he had known him, he had never deemed him suicidal, and concluded that there must be more to this than met the eye. He was relieved that the incident had happened *after* he had left Liverpool.

He had just eaten lunch when there was a knock on the door. It was a press photographer, and before he knew what was happening, a flashbulb popped in his face.

"Mr. Nelson," the reporter asked. "I wonder if might ask you a couple of questions?"

He was allowed get no further.

"I've nothing to say," Jake levelled. "I was here when it happened. Leave me be!"

He did not realise was that with this simple statement, he had said *too* much. The next morning when he went out to buy a newspaper, his face stared back at him from the front page, along with the headline:

WHO IS THE HANDSOME MYSTERY MAN AT THE CENTRE OF THE LENNIE STEVENS DEATH INVESTIGATION?

When Jake turned the corner to walk back to the bedsit, he observed a crowd of around twenty people standing outside the entrance to the building.

146

"There he is!" someone yelled.

Jake was deliberating what to do—whether to shoulder past the crowd, or to turn around and head off somewhere else—when a white Mini screeched to a halt in front of him, and the passenger door was flung open.

"Quick, Jake. Get in!"

It was Ricky. Now, things were happening *too* fast. Jake got in, and had barely closed the door when Ricky set off at break-neck speed, taking the next corner on two wheels and then pulling into a narrow side-street.

"Fuck me," Jake gasped. "I never knew you *had* a car!"

Ricky grinned, "I'll fuck you later, treacle. There's a lot of things about me you don't know. It's a good job I was there when I was, otherwise those buggers would have eaten you alive. I always suspected your Lennie Stevens was well-hung. Now I know he was!"

"And that's in very bad taste," Jake told him. "Where are you taking me?"

"To my place, and eventually to heaven," Ricky replied. "I just drove past Tommy Vincent's office. There must be a hundred people outside. Reporters…hysterical girls. The bloke was popular, I'll say that."

Two hours later, they were post-coital on Ricky's couch. Their love-making had been more hurried than they would have liked, but glorious nonetheless. Ricky's place was a first-floor flat on Rupert Street. It was small, comprising a living-room, kitchen, bathroom and bedroom, but still a far cry from what Jake had expected.

"Welcome to my humble abode," he had pronounced.

147

Jake felt guilty for having anticipated threadbare carpets, cheap linoleum, and a shared bathroom on the landing—not somewhere that had stepped straight out of the Ideal Home Exhibition. Whoever Ricky was, he had taste—and, Jake suspected, a wealthy sugar-daddy because there was no way he could afford such luxury from wanking off old men at ten-shillings a time!

Toying indolently with Ricky's spent cock, Jake's eyes took in the room. Besides the maroon, velour-covered three-piece suite there was a mahogany coffee-table and a sideboard, a tall unit containing cut-glass figurines, and an occasional table in front of the window upon which were two framed photographs—one of the America singer, Johnnie Ray, the other a member of the royal family.

"In answer to the question you're about to ask—yes, I have, with both of them," Ricky said. "Johnnie played the Palladium a few years back. We met in his dressing-room. The money he paid *me* to fuck *him* paid for this couch. He was uncircumcised, too. You don't usually get that with Americans. Every time he visits London, we get together. So, what's the story with you and Rory Storm?

Jake told him, "There isn't one. Well, maybe a little bit."

"But you *did* fuck each other?" Ricky pressed.

Jake shook his head and explained, "Rory said he didn't like taking it up the bum. After the session with Martha, there wasn't much fuel left in the tank. I wanked him off, he wanked me off. End of story. He's a nice bloke."

He nodded towards the royal picture and said, "Now it's my turn. What's the story with you and him?"

"Once a month," Ricky said. "Always the same routine. He calls it royal protocol. I fuck him after supper before we go to sleep, and he fucks me back when we wake up."

"And…he *pays*?" Jake asked.

"A hundred pounds a time," Ricky replied. "Mind you, I had to swear to be discreet, and I don't doubt that if word ever got out, I'd be found at the bottom of the Thames wearing concrete boots."

"Yet you don't charge me," Jake chuckled. "So, what's the difference between me—and Johnnie Ray and Prince Charming over there?"

Ricky reached across Jake for his cigarettes, and it just slipped out.

"I guess it's because I'm in love with you, and have been since our first night together…"

*

The next morning, Jake called Tommy Vincent to suss out the situation. Tommy informed him how the post-mortem had revealed that Lennie Stevens had hanged himself with his trouser-belt, though the hastily summoned inquest had been unable to ascertain why, when he had apparently been in such high spirits hours before his death. The receptionist at the Regency Hotel repeated what he had told the police—while Martha Longhurst was now claiming that, one hour before going down into the cellar, Lennie had asked her to marry him.

"We were *so* in love," Martha was quoted as having told

149

one Sunday newspaper. "Lennie was planning a Christmas wedding. Now, I have nothing."

"It's all a mess," Tommy told Jake over the phone. "I'm opening the office tomorrow, and there'll always be something for you here—*besides* fucking me over the end of the desk. I do think though that you should take some time off until after the funeral, to stop tongues wagging."

The papers were still having a field-day. Had Martha made up the story about the marriage proposal? Had Lennie got her pregnant, and killed himself to avoid facing the scandal? And, one tabloid queried, had the singer nurtured "unnatural physical tendencies", and taken his life because someone had been blackmailing him with exposure to the press? The fact that there were two smaller photographs under his—one of a snarling Jake snapped from the door of his bedsit, the other of Tommy—suggested one thing.

"They're speculating that we were shagging one other," Jake told Ricky, over breakfast. "Well, where Tommy and me were concerned that's certainly true. But Lennie and me? I wouldn't have touched him with a bargepole!"

"You had a threesome, of sorts," Ricky mused. "Wasn't there one teensy-weensy moment when you wanted it to go further—you know, when you were giving Martha one and he was sitting in the chair, tossing himself off?"

"No," Jake replied. "I have to admit that watching him made it all the more exciting with her. I may even have shut my eyes for a minute and imagined I was stuck inside him. But the bloke was so fucking horrible."

"He'll have a big funeral," Ricky said. "According to the

150

news, no date's been set other than it's next week. It looks like you're going to have a little time on your hands, baby. I was thinking, maybe we should have a little holiday. Nothing too elaborate. Why don't you think about it while I'm having a shower?"

Jake had already thought about it, and while Ricky was in the bathroom called Mark, who sounded a little peeved.

"I've read the papers," drawled. "Just because you're in the big city, you don't have to pretend I've been banished to Siberia. I saw your picture in the paper. Are you missing me, Jake?"

"That goes without saying," Jake replied. "I'm thinking it might be a good idea if we paid you a visit—you know, to catch up?"

"*We*?" Mark posed.

Jake told him, "His name's Ricky and he's—well I guess the best word would be adorable."

He opted not to mention Ricky's profession, or that he had told him he loved him.

"He's eager to meet you," he said. "Very much so…"

"You mean you've told him I'm a fantastic hairy-arsed fuck, and he wants to try me out?" Mark chortled. "Well, you know me well enough to know I'll try anything once. When do you plan on coming up here?"

Jake told him some time during the week, and a moment later hung up. He was still chuckling to himself when Ricky returned from the bathroom, naked and towelling his hair dry, the vigorous movement causing his huge cock to sway from side to side like a fleshy pendulum.

"I caught the tail end of that," he said. "What are you up to, Jake?"

"I called Mark." Jake explained. "You were the one who said I had time on my hands. I told him I'm going back up there for a few days, and that you'd be coming with me."

"*That'd* be a first," Ricky put in with a saucy grin. "We haven't quite perfected the art of simultaneous orgasm, but we're getting there."

"You know what I mean," Jake levelled. "I said we'd be *travelling* up there together. But if you're not free, I'm okay staying here…"

Ricky silenced him with a kiss, and said, "Of course I'll come with you. Mark sounds like a fun bloke. But you're not driving us up there in the Rolls, are you? We might be better with my Mini, taking turns driving."

Jake informed him they would be going by train—his treat. The next morning, Monday, he called Tommy.

"The funeral's Thursday," Tommy said. "Take the whole week off. Tony Manila's minder's just given notice, so you'll be driving him around when you get back—that's if you want the job."

"A dodgy character if ever there was one," Ricky told him, when Jake explained about the new job. "Tony Manila takes it up the bum like the best of them, so I've heard, but he's rumoured to have been hand-in-glove with the Krays…and he's got a boyfriend who'd cut your throat as soon as look at you. It's none of my business, treacle, but if I were you I'd definitely give that one a wide berth."

152

10: Back To Yorkshire

July-August 1964

It was after nine when they arrived at Doncaster railway station, and Jake thought of giving Mark a call from the phone-box in the entrance hall and asking him to pick them up. Then he recalled his trips to the station when living in these parts—a double-decker bus which took in every village along the way and which he had hated, but which would afford Ricky to see a little colour after the drabness of London. They completed their journey by foot, tramping down the tree-lined narrow lane to Mark's cottage—which, had they continued, would have taken them up the hill to Partridge Farm.

When Jake had left this place, it had been under a cloud. Then he had been terrified of public opinion, of bumping into one of the local scandalmongers. Now, he didn't care. He was happy. The man walking next to him—holding his hand because there was no one around—had told him that he loved him, and he was starting to feel the same way.

The cottage was in total darkness, and a note was pinned to the door, the contents of which Jake could just make out in the fading light:

> J. HAD TO GO TO WHITBY. WILL CALL &
> EXPLAIN. KEY IN USUAL PLACE. M.

"Wait here," he told Ricky. "Shan't be a sec…"

He found the key under a brick in the back yard and they

let themselves in. Ricky shivered. When they left London the city had been enjoying a heatwave, but walking into the cottage was like walking into a fridge.

"Thank God I've somebody to cuddle up to, tonight!" he told himself.

Jake flicked on the living-room light, and closed the curtains. Mark had left a bucket of coal next to the hearth, along with newspapers and firewood. While the kettle was boiling on the gas stove in the kitchen, Jake got a fire going and the room soon warmed up. There were tins and packets in the larder, and he cobbled together a simple meal. Tomorrow they would go shopping. What fun he envisaged *that* would be, facing the locals for the first time since leaving here…and with a man whom everyone would know was his boyfriend!

"There's so much prejudice here," he told Ricky while they were eating, each with his own armchair in front of the fire, which they had had allowed to die down now that the room had been warmed through. "I never realised what a backwater it was until I'd spent time somewhere else. A bloke can cheat on his missus and kick the shit out of her when he comes home from the pub, but woe betide anybody that's living over the brush—worse still if they have kids out of wedlock. As for men like us—in the old days they'd have strung us up from the nearest lamp-post. God, that was in bad taste. Poor old Lennie…"

They finished eating, and afterwards shared a bottle of wine which Jake found in the larder. He would replace it tomorrow though he couldn't think of any shops in the area

154

that sold wine—or any pubs, for that matter, so he figured he would buy Mark a bottle of whisky instead.

"My old man used to say that only Froggies and queers drank wine," he told Ricky. "In these parts, if you don't get slaughtered on ale every now and then and get involved in a scrap, there's summat wrong with you."

Soon afterwards, they went up to bed—to a bed which was like an ice-box. In London they had slept in their skin, but here, even in July, they kept on their underpants and T-shirts, and within minutes of cuddling up to each other under the blankets, they were sound asleep.

When Ricky stirred the next morning—courtesy of a stray cockerel that had wandered into the back yard and opted to crow directly under the window—he fumbled in the bed next to him to find an empty space. He couldn't remember exactly what he had been dreaming about, save that a punter had been involved and he had ended up in this house, freezing cold even in summer, and instead of having sex they had talked about murder! For a few terrifying seconds, he wondered if it *had* been just a dream. This man had brought him here to bump him off! Then he slapped himself across the face, and brought himself back to reality. He got up and dressed, descended the stairs and entered the living room where a small fire was burning in the grate. A moment later Jake breezed in, with two mugs of tea. He was wearing denims and a tight-fitting T-shirt which highlighted his superbly muscular torso.

"Here you are, Mr. Ross," he pronounced. "Better get this inside you!"

155

Ricky grinned. He recalled having a raging hard-on, last night when getting into bed, and cursed himself for falling asleep before putting it to good use. Now he was feeling as horny as a goat.

"The tea can wait," he said. "Right now, there's only one thing I want inside me, and that's *you*, Mr. Nelson!"

Grabbing Jake by the belt, he pulled him towards him, unzipped his denims, and drew these and his underpants down to his knees. Jake's cock stiffened at once, and Ricky had taken the head into his mouth and was swirling his tongue around the sweet-tasting ridge when there was a ferocious hammering on the door.

"Shit," Jake exclaimed. "It's my old man. He must have come by and seen the note on the door..."

He pulled up his clothes, and grabbing a pullover which Mark had left lying around held this in front of him so that their unwelcome visitor, whoever it was, would not observe the bulge formed by the hard-on which Jake knew would not subside until he had emptied his balls. It was not Eddie, however, but a policeman.

"Hello, Mr. Nelson," he posed. "I'm Constable Collins ...Jeff. Would it be okay if I came in?"

Jake moved to one side as he stepped inside the passage, then looked outside to see if his father was there. He wasn't, and he showed the policeman into the living-room where Ricky was sitting on the edge of his armchair, sipping his tea and looking all innocent.

"Is there somewhere we can talk privately?" the officer asked, looking about him.

Jake told him, "Anything you have to say can be said in front of my friend. I suppose this is about the money? Well, it's of any interest, I never touched a penny. It's all in the bank and he can have it back."

Jeff half-smiled and responded, "I think you'd better sit down, Mr. Nelson—Jake. I have some bad news…"

Jake blanched, but he did not sit down. Something bad had happened to Mark, he was sure. Why else would a copper come banging on the door, if it had nothing to do with the money he had stolen?

"Mark," he began. "Just tell me and get it over with…"

"Mark's fine," Jeff conformed. "I saw him in the pub the other evening. He said he was going to Whitby—something about a job on the trawlers. Jake, it's your dad. There's no easy way of saying this—"

"Then just say it and put us out of our misery," Ricky chimed in.

Jeff explained, "There was an accident—Tuesday night, up at the farm. Your dad's dead. He was found yesterday morning, first thing. We didn't know who to contact, what with your brothers being in Australia. Then I thought of Mark—maybe if he hadn't set off for Whitby yet, he might know where I could get in touch. Then I saw the note on the door just now. If I might be so bold, you don't look that shocked."

"Should I be?" Jake shrugged, though he *was* stunned. "Mark told me about him coming here with a bobby and yelling the place down, making all kind of threats."

"I know all about that," Jeff said. "I was the bobby. I've

known Eddie for years. He wasn't the nicest of men, that much I can say…"

He paused, as Ricky handed him a cigarette.

"Du Maurier," he mused. "These are a bit fancy for these parts. Thanks."

"So, what happened?" Jake asked. "No doubt he was pissed off his head?"

"It appears so," Jeff replied. "One of the farm labourers found him at the bottom of the stairs. It looks like he took a tumble and banged his head against the wall. There'll be a post-mortem, more than likely. The police doctor says he wouldn't have suffered—"

"More's the pity," Jake could not help but chime in. "So, what happens now?"

Jeff enlightened him, "He's been taken to the morgue in the village. Somebody will have to formerly identify him. Unfortunately that's going to have to be you. Will you be here at—shall we say, two o'clock?"

Jake nodded, and a moment later Jeff shook hands with him and Ricky, and left.

"That one's a bit of all right," Ricky observed, as they stood at the window and watched Jeff striding towards the gate. "Sorry about your dad, Jake. I know he sounds a bit of a turd, but he *was* your dad…"

"Balls," Jake snarled. "You don't know what the bloody hell you're talking about."

He realised at once that he should not have snapped, and wrapped an arm about Ricky's waist and kissed the crown of his head.

"Sorry," he soothed. "That was mean of me. Eddie might have sired me, but as far back as I remember he's behaved like an out-and-out twat. I'm not glad he's dead, but I'd be a hypocrite if I felt even slightly upset. I'm actually looking forward to going to the morgue to identify him. That way I'll definitely know the old bastard's dead."

They moved away from the window. Ricky was feeling despicably horny, and desperate to continue what they had started before being interrupted—but not sure that sucking Jake's cock was the right thing to be doing minutes after finding out that his homophobic father had cashed in his chips. Five minutes later, they were heading for the shop in the village, and Jake seemed to have forgotten about his father already.

"I swear to God I'll snog you right on the gob if anybody says anything," he told Ricky as they were walking through the door.

In fact the shop was empty and the usual assistant—Jake had bedded her last year while her husband had been away on a fishing trip—wasn't working today. In her place was a middle-aged woman he hadn't seen before. He filled his basket, paid for his purchases which included the bottle of Scotch for Mark, and they left.

"I feel disappointed," Jake said, as they turned into the lane leading to the cottage. "I was looking forward to the shop being full of fishwives, and giving them summat to gawp at. Might even have got you to fuck me over the end of the counter. That was a joke, by the way."

Jake made sandwiches for lunch, and they were sitting at

the kitchen table eating these when the phone rang. It was Mark, whose deep drawl sent shivers down Jake's spine.

"I heard the bad news," he said. "Or maybe that should that be the good news. Jeff called. He tells me this Ricky bloke's a looker…said that you scrub up well, too."

"Jeff," Jake pondered. "You said you were seeing one of the boys in blue. I assumed he'd be a sailor…"

"Oh, there's plenty of those up here in Whitby," Mark chuckled. "You'll find that out for yourself if I get the job and you come up here. Then again, you've got Ricky."

Jake was pleased that Ricky was still in the kitchen, finishing his lunch.

Lowering his voice, he said, "You know that Whitby's always been my dream. When are you coming back here, Mark?"

Mark told him, "That's it, Jake. I'm not sure. If I get the job I don't think I *will* be coming back—only to pack up my belongings, which hopefully will include you, and put the place up for sale. And things are all at sixes and sevens with you down in London now that loopy Lennie's topped himself. Think about it, Jake. You and me. We could have a good life up here. Oh, and there's something else. The next time you see Jeff, tell him that I've said you're to give him a good seeing to. He'll like that. It's always a good thing to keep on the right side of the law."

With this Mark hung up and Jake returned to the kitchen where Ricky was at the sink, washing up.

"He's incorrigible," Jake told him. "You'll never guess what he's just asked me to do, and with a bobby!"

160

Ricky was about to respond, when there was a tap on the door—Jeff Collins, earlier than expected. He was wearing civvies—blue denims, a checked shirt, and sneakers. Jake, who opened the door, could only catch his breath.

"My shift finished half an hour ago," he announced. "If it's okay with you, I'd like to get this done with. I've been a copper for three years now but morgues still freak me out. My car's parked at the top of the lane."

Jake locked the door and shoved the key into his pocket, and the trio headed up the lane, with Jake feeling elated and more than a little apprehensive after what Mark had said.

"The next time you see Jeff, tell him that I've said to give him a good seeing to…"

Jeff was handsome enough—tall and blond, big brown eyes, and what looked like a decent set of muscles under that shirt. But he was a *policeman*, and you just did *not* go propositioning policemen with offers of sex!

The morgue was a tiny brick building next to the canal. Jake's mother had often said that if Eddie ever got drunk once too often on his way back from the Rainbow—his alternative watering-hole just down the road—and tumbled into the water, they wouldn't have far to carry him. The place reeked of antiseptic, and whoever had brought Eddie here had not made an effort to make him look decent. He lay on a slab, still wearing the grimy overalls Jake assumed he had died in. A blood-stained cloth was wound around the top of his head, and one eye was wide open.

"That's him," Jake muttered. "Now can we go?"

They set off back to the top of the lane in Jeff's car, and

161

Jeff asked Jake if he had given any thought to the funeral arrangements, bearing in mind his brothers were thousands of miles away and yet to be contacted—that he *was*, in their absence, Eddie's next-of-kin.

"They can leave him where he is for all I care," he said. "I've come all the way up here to avoid one funeral, so I'll be buggered if I'm going to hang around for another. He has a sister in town. She knew him before we did. Let *her* do all the honours."

Jeff followed them into the cottage, and hung back in the doorway, deliberating whether to stay or leave.

"I had a phone call earlier, from Mark," Jake told him. "It was about you…"

"He called me too," Jeff responded, apprehensively. "He told me—"

He got no further, as Jake pulled him into the passage, slammed the door shut and backed him up against the wall.

"It's so inappropriate, though," Jeff got out, as their lips collided. "I mean, you're supposed to be in mourning for your father…"

Jake reached down and cupped one around Jeff's groin.

"Who's as stiff right now as you are," he mused.

Seconds later he had unzipped him and fished out his cock, and was leading him—by this—into the living-room, where Ricky had already stripped down to his underpants.

"Looks like I'm going to be getting two for the price of one," Jeff said, staring at the grapefruit-sized bulge before kicking off his shoes and unbuttoning his shirt.

Ricky sank to his knees in front of him, and coursed the

162

tip of his tongue around Jeff's thick, uncut cock. It tasted a little musky, but this he did not mind. He had tasted worse, and in any case after a little while it was as it should have been and drooled a little precum which Ricky devoured before plowing down further and taking him to the back of his throat. Then, when Jeff's groans suggested he might be getting ready to explode, Ricky stopped fellating him and stood up. Jeff stepped back, and quickly undressed.

"Wow," Jake gasped. "You were spot on, Ricky. He *is* a bit of all right..."

Jeff was blessed with a broad chest with an average smattering of trimmed, light brown bristles—a pretty little love-trail, and dense pubes which complimented his sturdy, but not specifically lengthy cock. What impressed them the most was the size of his scrotum, the way it hung heavy and loose between his muscular thighs, as if someone had filled it with lead.

"Those balls are going to produce one hell of a load," Ricky said. "What do you think, Jake?"

Jake was yet to undress. Moving behind Jeff, he began nibbling the back of his neck, executing little pecks all the way down his spine, but stopping when he reached the fluffy hairs around his tailbone. He had rimmed Ricky, but only in the shower or immediately afterwards. He had eaten out Tommy because Tommy had reassured him the larder had just had a good wash. Jeff had just come off his shift, and it didn't seem polite to ask him to nip upstairs and give his arse a scrub. But oh, what a *gorgeous* arse! Bubble cheeks smooth as a new-born baby's...hairy as a windswept plateau when he crouched to spread them and blow cool air against the shiny, tight-puckered hole.

"He looks way, way too tight," he was thinking himself. "Neither of us are going to get our cocks in there without making him yelp…"

And Ricky was saying, as he fondled Jeff's balls, "Well, Constable—which of us is going to be first?"

He stepped out of his briefs, and his cock flopped free, not quite fully erect but enough to make Jeff eyes almost stand out on stalks. Then when Jake undressed and he saw the size of *his* equipment, Jeff swallowed hard. What a choice to make! Jake, the Titan farmer's boy with muscles in his spit…and Ricky, the Cockney rebel with the smile to die for. And both of them hung like dray-horses.

"Now that I've seen the size of your weapons, neither of you," he pronounced with the stern authority of an upholder of the law. "But I *am* going to do you both, if that's okay?"

Ricky shrugged his shoulders and quipped, "That's fine by me? What do you say, Jake?"

Jake's response was to prostrate himself on the rug in front of the hearth. In this very cottage he had lost his man-with-man virginity to Mark. He had yet to make love to Ricky in this special place—their foreplay this morning had been interrupted by this cocky policeman, who at the time he had wanted to thump senseless. Now he wanted *hump* him senseless…

"Not on the rug," Jeff told him. "The last time Mark and me did the business on the rug, something shot out of the fire and burned my arse."

164

"Easily remedied," Jake grinned, getting up and rushing into the kitchen, returning with a wire fireguard, though the fire was almost out. "There. And you'll be needing this."

Dipping into the pocket of his discarded denims, Ricky produced a tiny bottle of lubricant.

"Jake told me all about Mark's antiquated methods," he said. "Sticky Vaseline that makes a mess of your arse and takes ages to wash off your cock. Down in London we do things more eloquently."

He passed the bottle to Jeff, and got down on to all fours on the rug. Jeff uncapped the tube, sniffed it, then swashed a liberal amount of lube around Ricky's hole and proceeded with a little gentle fingering. Though Jeff's cock was only around six inches in length, its girth was impressive and when he slammed home, Ricky yelped out.

"Shit, I didn't expect you to shove your bloody arm up there as well," he got out. "Go steady, man…"

Jeff had no intention of "going steady", though after a moment or two the discomfort turned to intense pleasure. Pulling up an armchair, Jake plonked himself down, spread his long legs wide, and began stroking. This was the first time he had watched anyone having sex, and sitting here just a few feet from the action turned him on beyond belief. After just a few minutes, though, he had to stop and sit on his hands—it was either that or blow before the other two had even got started.

Jeff was not a gentle lover, but he was an exciting one—gripping Ricky's middle so tightly that his fingernails dug into his ribs, fucking ferociously as his huge ball-pouch slapped against Ricky's perineum. In this position Ricky was unable to reach his own cock for fear of losing his balance—and he *so* needed to burp the baby, convinced that between them, Jeff and Jake would soon get him hard again. Then Jeff slowed down, edging as much as he dared before withdrawing his cock and rising to his feet, almost in slow motion. Staggering across to Jake, he managed to get between his outstretched thighs before blasting his load, four gushers which doused Jake's pecs.

For a moment, Jeff stood still, as if ejaculating had sent him into a trance. Jake smirked and stood up, Jeff's copious load coursing towards his pubes.

"You need to be bloody-well taught a lesson for making such a mess," he barked. "Down on your knees Mr. Plod!"

Jeff had really wanted to fuck the big farmer's boy who he had often seen strutting through the village yet not given a second thought about until this morning. He was however aware that it might take time for his balls to replenish after such an orgasm. Like Ricky, now occupying the chair Jake had vacated, he got down on all fours and only hoped that Jake would not give him the trouncing that *he* had just given Ricky, who now passed Jake the bottle of lube.

"I won't be needing that," Jake gruffed, spreading Jeff's cakes wide apart.

There was enough sweat here, he was sure, to guarantee him a comfortable ride. And *what* a deliciously hairy crack, just as he had come to like them—*so* hairy that he had to thumb the tendrils aside to locate Jeff's hole. Then, just to be extra-reassured of a smooth entrance, he scooped Jeff's

166

jism from his chest and abs and daubed this around the now pulsating ring muscle. Jeff *was* tight, and Jake didn't fancy poking his fingers in there so he pressed his helmet against Jeff's sphincter, pushed hard, and after a little not so gentle persuasion it gave way. Jake slid home, not stopping until his pubes were cushioned against Jeff's tailbone.

"Wow," he panted. "It doesn't feel that big now you've shoved inside me…"

The power of Jake's first few thrusts catapulted Jeff forwards all the same, and he would have ended up flat on his face, with Jake on top of him, had it not been for Ricky who got up out of the chair and grasped Jeff's shoulders to hold him steady. Ricky's load was still intact, but he had started to drool, not a drop of which was wasted as Jeff opened wide and swallowed not just Ricky's bell-end, but the better part of his rock-hard shaft. They stayed in this position for a good ten minutes—Jake moving slowly, his big strawberry glans nudging against Jeff's prostate, and with Jeff attempting to fellate the life out of Ricky and enjoying the sweet-salty tang of pre-cum. The phone rang, making them jump and almost causing Jake to disengage, but they ignored it and kept on humping and sucking. Then, when he sensed that Jeff's greedy gullet was maybe getting him a little too close to the brink, Ricky stepped back. For a few minutes more he sat on the edge of the armchair and watched Jake rutting like a stud bull, his face contorting as he tried to hold on to his climax.

"Time to have another piece of the action, methinks," Ricky pronounced, getting up again off the chair.

167

Scooting underneath two pairs of long, muscular legs, Ricky lay on his back and for a moment enjoyed the spectacle of his lover's third leg moving in and out of one of the hairiest arseholes he had ever seen—so hairy that the thick dark ropes adhered halfway along Jake's turgid shaft. Every now and then Jake withdrew, enabling Ricky to stretch up and flick his tongue against the underside of his helmet, sending him almost insane with the urge to shoot, yet still hanging on. Ricky licked one pair of tightening balls and then the other, before bending Jeff's hard-again cock downwards. With little difficulty he was able to take most of this in his gullet, and seconds later Jeff exploded once more—not a copious expulsion like the last one, but violent enough for him to cause Jake to slip out of him just as he was getting ready to shoot, the good half-dozen milky ropes drenching Ricky's face, throat and chest.

A moment later, Jeff and Jake had returned to the land of the living, and were lying side by side on the sheepskin rug, spent and heaving. Ricky towered above them, legs apart as he wanked furiously—seconds later letting go of his cock and allowing it to pump out his load of its own volition while he swayed his hips like a go-go dancer to ensure that each sweat-streaked torso got an equal dousing. When he was finished, Jake shifted to one side so that he could lie on the rug between them. Not long afterwards, they drifted off to sleep.

It was after six when Jake awoke. Ricky was snuggled on the rug next to him, snoring gently, but Jeff was gone.

11: Justin

August 1964

The next morning they had finished breakfasting when Jake reached across the table, took hold of Ricky's hand, and turned it palm-upwards as if he reading his fortune.

"Ricky, I've been mulling this thing over for a couple of days now," he said. "I've come to an important decision."

Ricky cracked a lop-sided smile, the kind that always sent shivers down his spine.

"Don't tell me—you're going to have a sex change," he responded. "All those women, and now going at it with other blokes like you invented being queer. Go ahead. It wouldn't stop me loving you and it certainly wouldn't stop me wanting you. I'd just have to use a different hole…"

"Shut up," Jake rapped. "I'm being serious. I've decided to go to the old bastard's funeral this afternoon. Actually, it was Mark's idea the last time he called. He thinks it'll bring closure. I also called Tommy while you were in the shower. They're burying Lennie this morning. How's about that— two of the most horrible people I've ever known, being potted on the same day."

Ricky hated to hear him talking about Mark, though he would never have told Jake this, and it had taken a lot of getting used to—eating in Mark's home, sleeping in his bed, having sex in his living-room. Tomorrow they would be returning to London, and normality. Mark, as nice as he sounded, would hopefully be assigned to Jake's past.

"He's right," Ricky told him. "You *should* go. But what

169

about all your relatives, all those nosey parkers? There'll be a lot of funny stares, a lot of tongues wagging if this place is as judgemental as you say it is."

Jake shrugged his shoulders, and continued stroking his lover's hand.

"I'll just have to try and ignore them," he replied. "It'd be nice if Pete and Paul could be there, but so far as I know they haven't been told yet. In any case, how would they get here from Melbourne at such short notice? So—are you coming with me?"

Ricky chortled at this, "And *really* give them something to talk about? No, treacle. You've gone through enough trauma without having that. I'll just toddle off for a walk somewhere and take a look at the landscape. You *are* okay going on your own?"

Jake nodded and promised him that he would be fine. He realised there would be considerably more than the funeral to deal with. After today, something would have to be done about the farm. He wasn't sure whether his father would have left a will, but he knew he wouldn't be able to return to London just yet. While Ricky was clearing the table, he called Tommy and explained his change of plan.

"You just caught me," Tommy said. "I'm about to leave for the church. We still don't know where Lennie lived. Would you believe that? Martha's been saddled with all the arrangements and the cortege starts off at the funeral home. Bury your dad and fuck your boyfriend, Jake, preferably in that order. The one will relieve the stress of the other. And don't worry about rushing back here. I reckon I can manage without you for another week. Mind you, I am going to miss than big cock of yours."

Jake hung up. Eddie's funeral was not until two, but he realised he had nothing to wear other than the few things he had brought with him. His suit and his other clothes were, he assumed, still hanging in the wardrobe at Partridge Farm —unless Eddie had thrown them out.

*

To say that Eddie Nelson had been disliked by just about everyone in the village, a lot of people turned up for his funeral—the sister he hadn't spoken to in five years, two cousins Jake could not remember ever seeing before—all of these hypocrites dabbing their eyes at the graveside. The elements too seemed to be in mourning. It had been fine all day, but as they were lowering the coffin into the ground the sky turned grey, then black, and the heavens opened. Jake muttered an obscenity. The vicar was rambling on about saving souls and forgiving even the blackest sins—no doubt unaware that a few years ago, Eddie, the archetypal agnostic, had been sniffing around his wife. Jake closed his eyes as the rain smacked against his face, plastered his hair against the top of his head, not praying but seeing the image of himself as a child, and his father stomping into the house in a drunken rage, and laying into him and his mother just for the hell of it.

From the cemetery, the mourners headed for the church hall where a spread had been organised. Jake had just taken his place at the table when Aunt Lucy, Eddie's estranged sister, marched up and tapped him on the shoulder.

"Come back to see what we can scrounge, have we? If Eddie had any sense, he'll have left the farm to me, what with two sons buggering off to Australia and the other one buggering off to—well, to London to get buggered."

A few of the mourners sniggered at this. Jake ignored them. He wasn't hungry in any case, so he got up and went outside for a smoke. The rain had stopped, and he was standing under the porch enjoying his cigarette when his cousin Justin—Lucy's youngest son—sidled up to him.

"I heard Mother just now," he said. "I've been hearing all sort of stories about you. You know, about how you've decided to leave the ladies alone so you can take it up the shitter. What does it feel like, *Jakey*, having a knob shoved up your arse?"

Jake nodded to the outbuilding, where the groundsmen kept their tools.

"Why don't we go in there, and see how long it takes to find out?" he posed. "I promise to be gentle, *Justine*."

Justin smirked and sloped off, and Jake decided to leave everyone to their fake tears and boiled ham and head back to the farm. Until now he had not given much thought to what might happen to the place which held so many horrid memories. He assumed it would definitely *not* go to Aunt Lucy, but to his brother Paul, seeing as he was the eldest.

The house felt as welcoming as a tomb and as he turned the key in the lock behind him, Jake shuddered to think that for twenty years he had called this place home. There were two large suitcases in his father's room, and he took these into his bedroom and filled them with clothes and personal effects. Everything was exactly as he had left it, which gave him the expression that Eddie might have been expecting him to come back, all apologetic and with his tail tucked between his legs. He was wishing now that he had driven up here in the Rolls instead of taking the train—there would have been enough room in the boot and the back seat to pack everything, instead of having to be selective. Then he chuckled to himself, wondering what the hypocrites at the church hall would have had to say about *that*! Now, he faced the prospect of tramping across the fields and down to Mark's cottage loaded up like a pack-horse.

He was about to leave, when he had a sudden thought. What if Eddie had stashed away some more money? He hated the idea of stealing from the dead, but if anyone else found it—Aunt Lucy for instance—he was sure they would do the same. He went back into Eddie's room and looked in the dressing-table. Sure enough there was a stash in the Cadbury's Chocolate Fingers tin—not as much as before, but almost a hundred pounds. Then he opened the top drawer. His mother's jewellery was there, what few pieces she had possessed—the eternity ring which had belonged to her own mother, two bracelets, a gold locket containing her picture, and a sapphire brooch. There was no way, Jake told himself, that anyone else would be getting their hands on these. He shoved them into his pocket, and hurried down the stairs with the suitcases. He had just locked the door when he saw his cousin Justin heading up the path.

"One word out of you, shit-face, and I'll have to make a decision whether to break both your arms or just one," Jake growled, bunching his fists.

Justin smiled—then lunged at Jake and, grabbing him by the arm manhandled him back towards the house. Jake was impressed. Justin had always seemed the family weakling, despite being six-feet tall and sportingly built.

"So," Jake got out. "You want to fight? Bring it on…"

"I want to do no such thing," Justin growled, letting go of Jake's arm. "I wasn't taking the piss, what I said about you taking it up the arse. I was genuinely curious…anxious to find out. There aren't many blokes like us around these parts. I keep asking Davey to try, but he reckons it's dirty to shove it where the shit comes out."

Jake's eyes opened wide, but before he could respond, Justin backed him up against the door. Their lips collided.

"Blokes like *us*? he panted, when they came up for air. "Davey? Davey Watson—your best mate at school?"

Justin explained, with some satisfaction, "Didn't see that one coming did we, Jakey? Davey and me have been living together for more than a year. Not here, obviously. We've a little place in town. He teaches at the grammar school, same as me. We'd get the sack if anybody found out."

All of a sudden Jake was sweating like a horse. Justin, the family milksop—and Davey Watson, the school stud!

"Davey had four or five different lasses while we were in the fifth form," Jake said, still not believing what he was hearing. "Some Fridays after school some of us would pay him sixpence apiece to go off into the wood and watch him

174

fucking one of them. And you're trying to tell me he's—"

"A bender?" Justin suggested. "If I remember rightly, you've had more than your share of fanny, and you ended up with Mark Noble. Well, that's what folk around here are saying. The family made it quite clear they didn't want *him* at the funeral, but it seems like he's vanished off the face of the earth. Well, to Whitby, some folk are saying."

"Some folk are saying a lot," Jake mused.

Justin kissed him again, this time more gently.

"So, who's this Cockney bloke you're shacked up with, Jakey?" he asked.

Jake dug into his pocket for the key, unlocked the door, and pulled Justin inside. The last thing he wanted was for Aunt Lucy to appear on the scene and see him snogging her pride and joy on the front step.

"That's Ricky," he said. "I wouldn't say I'm shacked up with him, though. We came up here to get away from all the publicity down in London. Lennie Stevens' funeral was today, too."

"I read that in the paper," Justin said. "Saw your picture. You weren't bending him as well, were you?"

Jake laughed loudly at this and retorted, "If you'd met him, you wouldn't be asking that question. The man was vile. He—"

Justin pushed him back against the wall, the very one which had sent Eddie Nelson to meet his Maker—the dried bloodstain was still there—silenced him with another kiss, and then reached down to grope his crotch.

175

"Stop talking, Jakey," he breathed in his ear. "Since I saw you standing at the graveside I've been lusting after you. And I know you want to…"

Jake very much wanted to, and could not lock the door fast enough and head for upstairs. It excited him that he was going to have sex for the first time in the bed that he had only ever wanked in—that last time fantasising about Mark. But Mark—and Ricky—were not on his mind right now as his libido took over. His cousin was cute, and it had taken him until now to realise *how* cute: dark curly hair, nut-brown eyes surmounted by shaggy brows, just a hint of stubble on his dimpled chin and angular cheeks, full almost feminine lips. He was unsure that he should be getting physical with a relation. Then he reminded himself of two things, as his heart started pounding. Firstly, Justin was a man and hardly likely to get up the duff—secondly, he was adopted, and therefore *not* a blood relative.

In the bedroom, they stripped to their underpants, and lay facing each other on top of the bed. Justin had once seen Jake working in the field with his shirt off, and had known what to expect. The last time Jake had seen Justin minus clothes had been in the school gym, where the other boys had taunted him and called him "Tin-Ribs". The name certainly did not apply to him now. He had filled out and was almost as muscular as Jake—and had a splendidly hairy chest. For several minutes Jake was content just to lie there and hold him in his arms—and feel more than slightly ashamed of himself for having wanted to thump him. Then he rolled on top of him.

176

"I could kick myself," he murmured. "Why did we never get around to doing this before?"

Justin chuckled, "I suppose we could have, but I think Uncle Eddie might have had something to say if we'd done it here!"

Jake opted to take the lead, kissing Justin passionately while their crotches ground together. Moving downwards, he suckled each russet-pointed nipple, then poked the tip of his tongue inside his deeply-indented navel. Justin was wearing white briefs which revealed the outline of his rock-hard cock, and there was a wet patch where this had leaked. Jake licked around this, making the fabric translucent. Then he drew the briefs down over the dense black pubes, and Justin's weapon sprang free. It was not large—six inches maximum—and not particularly thick but Jake decided that it was a beautiful cock all the same. He worked the foreskin back over the glistening head, and Justin squirmed as Jake took this into his mouth. Closing his eyes, he thought of all that had happened since the last time he had ejaculated in this bed—the fucking and being fucked, the rimming, the cock sucking and the thrill of savouring a man's load for the first time—and the more he observed in his mind's eye, the harder he sucked on Justin's cock. Then, when Justin began groaning loudly, fearful that he might burp before he wanted him to, he spat out his meat, shimmied back up the bed and kissed him once more.

"You've got a very tasty tool, cousin," he mused, rolling on to his back and raising his hips to shrug out of his briefs.

Justine was gob-smacked, at what he was now seeing—

177

nine inches of solid, rope-veined meat stretching past Jake's navel, and he wasn't sure if it was fully erect! Jake read the concern on his face.

"It's up to you," he said. "I can give it or take it. If you don't want go all the way, we can toss one another off."

Justin swallowed hard, and decided that honesty was the best policy.

"I already told you, Davey doesn't go in for that kind of thing," he confessed. "He let me fuck him once, but he was drunk at the time. And I don't think…"

Jake allowed him to go no further, and as it looked like Justin was also nervous about sucking his cock—he had decided that despite his dishy looks, Davey Watson must be the most boring man in the world when it came to sex—he raised his knees until they were almost touching his chin.

"Spit in it," he said. "Poke around a little bit with your finger, if you like. If not, just press your bell-end against the hole and push hard. You've got me all sweaty so it'll go in without too much bother…"

Justin split Jake's cheeks like a melon. Such a beautiful arse, he told himself—a crack to die for with enough fur to knit a sweater—that spitting into it was akin to an act of sacrilege. Even so he hawked and delivered a gobbet smack in the centre of the winking bud, then proceeded as Jake had requested, his cock sliding home like a hot knife sinking into lard.

"Wow, that feels *so* nice, Jakey" he groaned. "I don't reckon I'm going to last long, though…"

"You will," Jake breathed. "If you feel like you're going

to fetch, just pull out and have a breather. It works for me every time."

Justin did this after just twenty or so thrusts, and risked inserting a finger. Jake moaned his appreciation of this, so he inserted another and wiggled them around. Then with his other hand he began stroking the thick log. He thought of asking Jake how he was doing, hoping that his lack of experience extant of mutual wanking and that singular fuck with Davey might not be too evident, but the almost sainted expression on Jake's face suggested that he was doing just fine. Removing his fingers, he replaced them with his cock. The urge to shoot had gone for now, and he shuddered as Jake reached behind him and spread his big hands about his rump, forcing him to thrust harder and deeper inside him. Justin yelped—but only by way of pleasure—as a long digit dug inside his sphincter, not stopping until it reached the third knuckle. Jake's finger-fucking was relentless, but astonishingly gentle—and a few minutes later as that finger located his prostate, Justin could hold back no longer.

"Let it go, baby," Jake drawled. "Let it go…"

Seconds later, Justin's hot load flooded his bowels, but even when he had finished ejaculating Jake would not let him withdraw, eager to explode while Justin was still hard and inside him. He began stroking furiously and was almost there when Justin playfully slapped the back of his hand.

"Please. Let me…"

Jake thrust his arms behind his head, exposing his black, sweaty pits. Justin wanked him slowly, and began moving inside him once more, wondering if he would be capable of

179

staying hard and going again—until Jake arched his back and ejaculated a perfect three-ribbon arc which catapulted into the middle of his chest. Justin reluctantly pulled out and lay next to him. The frantic fuck had temporarily exhausted them, and within minutes they were asleep.

When Jake awoke he panicked, sitting upright in the bed and gazing about him—at the old wardrobe, the blue velvet curtains, the bookcase in the corner, the dressing-table that had belonged to his grandmother. It had all been a dream— albeit a pleasant one! Mark and Tommy, Ricky, Justin...and the horrendous Lennie Stevens! Any minute now, his father would come hammering on the door, ordering him to get his arse out of bed, yelling that the cows were not going to milk themselves. Then he started to come to and, blinking himself back to reality, remembered what had happened— who it had happened with.

"Justin," he called out. "Where did you go?"

The door opened, and Justin walked in—he was naked, and didn't half look good!

"Call of nature," he mumbled, as Jake checked his watch and got out of the bed. "Where are you going, Jakey?"

"Shit," he exclaimed. "It's after six. Ricky's going to be wondering where I am!"

Justin coaxed him back on to the bed, and kissed him.

"Another half hour or so won't make much difference," he said. "Look what I found in the bathroom cabinet."

He opened his hand to reveal a tub of petroleum jelly.

"I really *do* want you to return the compliment, Jakey," he smiled. "I was thinking about it while I was watering the plants. If I can take that monster of yours, I can take anything from my Davey. You were certainly standing at the front of the queue when they were handing out cocks. So—what's with the face? Don't you want to?"

"Of course I *want* to," Jake told him. "It's that stuff. It's ghastly. In London they use stuff called lube, and it doesn't stink like engine oil. But, if you're sure..."

"Sure as eggs are eggs," Justin responded, rolling on to his front. "Just shove it in there. If it hurts, I'll probably scream like a stuck pig, but I know I'll like it..."

Again, Jake glanced at his watch. There was more than Ricky to consider. He had locked the door, but he was not the only one with a key. Supposing someone came—Aunt Lucy, for instance—and caught him fucking her son? Then he studied the firm, hairy and *very* appetising rump waiting to be serviced, and only wished that there might be all the time in the world...

"Hang on," he said. "Won't be a minute..."

It took him less than twenty seconds to rush downstairs to draw the bolts, and rush back to the bedroom. Straddling Justin's hips, he wedged his rock-hard cock between his cheeks, and at once located the gateway to heaven. Justin's hole was damp, but tight—very tight—and it took several attempts before he was able to work past the hard ring of muscle. More than once, Justin flinched.

"Tell me if it doesn't feel right," Jake murmured. "I can fetch very quickly if you want me to—or I can pull out if it hurts, and you can do me again. I don't mind. To say you haven't done much fucking, you're bloody good at it..."

181

Justin groaned, "Shut up talking, Jakey, and shag me. It feels great. Honest!"

Jake's other men had all liked it rough, but this one was different. He moved slowly inside him at first, balancing on his bunched fists so as not to feed him too much shaft until he was properly relaxed. Justin sensed his apprehension.

"Take it out, Jakey. Lie on your back…"

Jake did this, knowing all along that Justin would never be able to take it. Getting mounted by his cousin—by his *adopted* cousin—had been incredible and he was more than eager to feel Justin inside him once more. But Justin didn't want this. After encouraging Jake to lie on his back with his thighs together and his shoulders propped up by the pillows he straddled him so that they were facing…and while Jake held his cock steady, he slowly squatted down on him, not stopping until he had taken all nine inches, until he was in complete control of the situation.

"Davey's away at a teaching conference," Justin panted as he began bobbing up and down. "But I swear to God, tomorrow night while he's asleep I'm going to tie him to the bed. Then I'm going to wake him up and ride him till he blows like a whale. A sperm whale, ha!"

For Justin, this was paradise. Jake's cock was *massive*, yet it didn't feel in the least uncomfortable having all of it inside him. Jake could just as well have been fucking him with his finger, as he had earlier. And the man had staying power! Happy that Justin was good with his position, after a little while Jake began thrusting upwards, his huge helmet playing havoc with Justin's he assumed virgin prostate, and

182

with Justin shuddering each time his balls banged down against Jake's damp. springy pubes. Justin had started to drool, his pre-cum trailing a spittle line which swung from side to side before dripping on to Jake's belly. Reaching down, Jake wrapped one hand around the upright little cock, and gently as he could chafed the underside of his glans with the pad of his thumb. Gritting his teeth, Justin sprayed his load across Jake's chest, seconds before Jake lifted them both off the mattress and gushed his man-juice deep into his innards.

A moment later they disengaged, and for a few minutes lay side by side, panting and soaked with sweat. Justin's load tickled as it started coursing down Jake's side, but he had no desire to clean up. He was sure that if they stayed like this for half an hour or so, they would both be capable of going for the hat-trick. But he really did need to get back to Ricky. Reluctantly, he got up off the bed and dressed.

"Do you reckon we'll get to do this again?" he asked Justin, as they were leaving the house and they kissed one last time.

Justin nodded enthusiastically, "I'm sure of it. London's not exactly on the other side of the world, is it?"

With a spring in his step and half-walking, half-running, Jake headed back across the fields and down to the cottage. Not only did he feel great having spent the whole afternoon having sex with a man he had known his whole life, and who he never would have guessed was suitably inclined, he sensed that *he* had been the teacher. He would not get over the fact that his sixth form stud rival—Davey Watson—had like himself jumped over the fence and ended up living with another man. What amazed him more was that Davey had not jumped far enough. Justin may have only had a little cock compared to his own, but it had given just as much pleasure as Ricky's moosewhanger, and by refusing to let Justin stick it inside him, Jake was certain that Davey was missing out on a treat!

He was thinking about Ricky, wondering if he should tell him *why* he was late—that he had absconded from his father's funeral tea to fuck his adopted cousin—when he reached the cottage to find the door locked. He found the key in its usual place, under a brick in the back yard…and also found a note on the kitchen table, weighted down by the cruet. His heart sank as he read the contents:

> Dearest, darling Jake. Seeing you so settled in this cottage and overhearing you talking to Mark on the phone, I sense you're back where you belong. Mark called just after you left, and said it's now certain you'll be inhering a third share in the farm. No need for you to go back to London and drive tetchy pop stars around. No need either for me to go back to my old way of life. Knowing you, Jake, has enriched my life, and I hope in some little way knowing me has enriched yours. Just remember that I'll always love you. Ricky.

Jake took the note into the living-room, and slumped into chair Ricky had occupied this morning while they had been discussing their journey back to London. He was beyond tears. Half an hour ago he had felt on top of the world. His father was six feet under and no longer a threat. He didn't care about the farm, or what he and his brothers would do with it. He for one never wanted to live there again with all the bad memories and he was sure that Pete and Paul would feel the same way otherwise they wouldn't have made such an effort not just to leave there, but to head off to the other side of the world. Neither did he want to go back to London, unless to seek out Ricky and beg him to see sense, to make him realise that what they had was a deep and profound love and understanding of one another. The tone of the letter suggested, however, that Ricky didn't want this, that each of them had served his purpose and that it was now time to move on. But to *where*?"

There were a few packets of food left in the freezer, and at nine he fixed himself dinner. He thought about watching the television, but elected to go to bed instead. He awoke early the next morning, dressed and descended the stairs to put the kettle on. While sipping his tea, he reflected on recent events. The first time he had come to this cottage, he had been what Mark had called "a queer virgin"—his only experience that wank in the Storm House when they hadn't even touched each other. Since Mark there had been four others. Tommy Vincent, he knew, had shagged just about every man that had entered his office, but he and Jake had still grown fond of one another. Jeff had been a one-off, Justin too, though he really did hope that they would meet up again. Jake's progression into latent homosexuality had been gradual. Fucking had been the easiest aspect to get used to. That first time, Mark had told him not to look where he was shoving his cock, to pretend that he was a woman, that this would help him not to feel quite so edgy about penetrating a man. And he had taken to it like a duck to water! He had been apprehensive about sucking a cock for the first time, even more so about fingering, let alone rimming a man, and now he could not get enough of it! He had tasted and swallowed sperm! Yet he still found women attractive. The one-night stand with Martha had proved this, and only the other day a busty brunette had sat at the next table next to his in the greasy spoon at the end of his street. Such had been the effect when she smiled at him that had shoved his hand inside his trousers to straighten out his hard on before venturing to get up and leave.

Despite his burdening sadness, Jake chuckled to himself wondering—*if* he decided to stay here, as Ricky's note said he should—how difficult it might be luring Justin away from "wanking only" Davey Watson. He assumed not *too* difficult, but that doing so would be grossly unfair, if not inhuman, because there was considerably more to any relationship than just sex. Which left Ricky and Mark, *his* choice being that he could return to London and try and sort things out with the former—or he could follow his original dream and relocate to Whitby, where he and Mark could be together and start all over again. The shrilling of the telephone, while he was trying to work out what to do, provided him with the answer. It was Mark, who detected by the tone of Jake's voice that something was wrong.

"It's Ricky," he said. "I just got back from my old man's funeral, and he'd gone—just like that."

He explained some of what Ricky had written in his note —that if he hadn't been delayed after the funeral, he might have got back to the cottage in time to talk Ricky out of leaving. He didn't say *why* he had been delayed. Mark was very much to the point.

"Obviously, I feel for you," he soothed. "But I can't say that I'm sorry. I mean, a lovely bloke like you—living with a rent boy who's probably had his cock inside every other hole south of Watford Gap?"

Jake argued on this point, "We weren't *living* together. Ricky was talking about giving all that up. But now I've had a whole night to think things over, I'm thinking that maybe it *was* for the best. I was getting used to London, but it's not where I belong. Neither is this place—"

"Then come up here to me," Mark shot back. "I found myself a cosy little flat. It's not Buckingham Palace, but it's good enough for now. Once I've sold the cottage, I'm sure we'll be able to find somewhere better. Think about it, Jake. I have to go out in a few minutes, and I'm not sure when I'll be back. I'll call you first thing tomorrow. Maybe then you'll have an answer."

He hung up. Jake did not need to think about it for very long. Time and time again he had told himself there was nothing for him here. And what was waiting for him in London now, if Ricky really was gone from his life? What they had was good while it had lasted—more than good, it had been phenomenal. But after turning it over in his mind time and time again, Jake had come to the conclusion that Ricky was right. He *did* belong here—not in Brodsworthy, but certainly in the North among his own kind. Tommy had promised to keep him on, as a driver or as a bodyguard. But did he really want this, being at the beck and call of some other tetchy pop singer? More than this, a singer with alleged underground connections? And how long would his money last out? He had not touched his last wages, or the money in the bank—and he had the money he had filched yesterday out of Eddie's stash. But he knew that he would have dip into it sooner rather than later, and that when he did it, wouldn't last for ever.

12: Whitby

November 1964

They were happy. Like pigs in muck, Jake had told Justin, over the phone last week.

"Same here," Justin had said. "I carried out my threat—told Davey I had a headache, then waited until he was asleep and tied his hands and feet to the bedposts. I got him hard, straddled him, and once his cock was inside me and he'd woken up, I untied him and gave him a choice. Either I could ride him like there was no tomorrow, or I could climb off him and wank him off, like I'd been doing for the past twelve months. He told me to shut up and keep riding, and now he can't get enough of my arse. Haven't been inside his yet, but it'll happen..."

Jake had quit working for Tommy Vincent. On the first day of August last year, Mark had met him at the coach station in Whitby and taken him back to the flat. Two weeks later, a letter had arrived from Eddie Nelson's solicitor. Despite driving his three sons away from home, he had bequeathed the farm to them. Paul and Pete had contacted the solicitor, who had arranged for an estate agent to put the place up for sale, providing Jake was in agreement. It had taken two months to find a buyer, and the death duties had been steep. Even so, there had been a tidy sum to share between them.

Mark was working on the trawlers, which meant that he was sometimes away from home for two days at a time. Jake had hated this, at first, but had soon got used to it. Not

189

without difficulty, he had refrained from wanking during his lover's absence and because if this abstinence the sex, when Mark came home, was out of this world. On one occasion, Jake had surprised them both by ejaculating three times in one hour, without losing his hard on!

Five weeks ago, Jake had stared work at a food factory. It was far cry from driving around in a Rolls-Royce and he always stank like an otter when he got home, but it gave him something to do when Mark was absent, and would not be for ever. He had enrolled on a college course, set to start in the New Year, and would be studying to be a veterinary nurse specialising in livestock so he would still be involved with farming, in a manner of speaking. This morning he had called Justin to give him the good news—and to invite him and Davey Watson up to Whitby for the weekend. In his heart of hearts, now that Davey had "seen the light", so to speak, and with Mark at sea, he was hoping that the three of them might have a little fun together.

It wasn't Justin who answered the phone, however, but Aunt Lucy. Justin was too distressed to talk right now, she said. Two days ago, Davey had been working late at the grammar school, supervising detentions, and it had been dark when he had set off for home. While crossing the road, he had been knocked down by a car. Davey had died at the scene, and the driver had failed to stop.

"The police are looking for him," Aunt Lucy added. "As far as I'm concerned, killing that bastard did us all a favour. He turned my Justin into something he wasn't brought up to be. He turned him into a pervert like you."

Jake thought about asking Mark if he could borrow his car and drive down for Davey's funeral. Though he hadn't seen Davey in years, Justin would need a shoulder to lean on. Then he reminded himself what had happened the last time he and Justin had been reunited at a funeral, and came to the conclusion that it might be best to wait a while.

On 28 November, Jake turned twenty-one, though where some of his sexual partners were concerned—Jeff, Ricky, Rory—his twenty-first had been *last* year. He had lied about his age to his lovers because he had still been a minor and they could have gone to prison for having sex with him. Only Tommy Vincent had known the truth, having seen his driver's license—and Justin, who had turned twenty-one two months before Jake.

"The lusty Yorkshire farmer's lad's got muscles in his spit, he's hung like a bull and he fucks like he invented it," Tommy had written in his diary after they had sex for the first time. "Yet in the eyes of the law he's still a child. How ridiculous is that?"

*

Jake would never forget that late-November day—his birthday—as long as he lived…

Last night before they went to bed, Mark complained of feeling unwell, and again this morning when they awoke and Jake was sporting a boner which, Mark observed, looked solid enough to hammer nails into steel.

"Sorry, but I've got the most dreadful headache," he groaned, turning over and burying his face in the pillow. "Maybe if I lie in for a little while, it'll go off…"

191

Jake got up, went into the bathroom, and showered and shaved. He certainly hoped that Mark would be feeling fit by tonight, for they had booked a table at their favourite restaurant, overlooking Whitby harbour. Wrapping a towel about him, he went into the kitchen and put the kettle on. The dirty pots and glasses were still on the draining-board from last night. He put them into the sink, and was washing up when a pair of strong hands wrapped about his waist and began fumbling with the towel.

"Happy birthday, big boy," Mark murmured. "Time to give you your present, methinks!"

"You bugger," Jake chuckled. "You never *did* have a headache, did you?"

He half-turned. Mark was naked, his cock upstanding. Tied around it was a pink ribbon.

"Just keep facing the window, and think of England," Mark said. "Let *me* do the honours…"

The towel dropped to the floor. Jake was hard too, his cock squashed against the cold metal of the sink. Mark squatted on his haunches. Spreading Jake's cheeks wide, he pressed his lips against the damp, puckered bud and Jake shuddered as he tugged the strong black hairs surrounding it. Then Mark stood up, spat in the palm of his hand, and a moment later was inside him to the hilt. For a few minutes he moved rhythmically, one hand gently squeezing Jake's balls, the other stroking his log. Jake gritted his teeth and tried to hang on, aware that for him, morning sex rarely lasted very long. Outside, two police cars had pulled up— obviously something was happening in the street, but all he was interested in as Mark increased the power of his thrusts was the pistoning rod hammering against his prostate.

"Happy birthday, sweetheart," Mark growled, as with one almighty final lunge he raised them both on to their tiptoes and pumped out his load, while Jake screwed his eyes shut and blasted four spurts of jism into the sink, spattering the pots.

When he opened his eyes again, Jake looked out of the window and observed two policemen striding down the path towards the front entrance, followed by two burly men in suits.

"It'll be them upstairs again," he chuckled, meaning the occupants in the flat above them who never seemed to stop arguing. "Honestly, I can't understand why they don't just get a divorce, and give everybody a little peace..."

The police were not here to see the neighbours, and a moment later were hammering on the door of the flat. The lovers rushed back into the bedroom to grab their clothes. It was Jake who dressed first, and answered the door.

"Mark Noble?" one of the burly detectives posed.

"No, Mark's inside," he said. "What's all this about?"

He got to thinking again about the couple upstairs. The other day, when Mark had threatened to report them to the landlord about their arguing, mostly in the middle of the night and waking everybody up, *they* had threatened to report Mark and Jake for their "deviant sexual practices".

"We've done nothing wrong," Jake blurted out, staring at Mark's pink ribbon, on the floor. "I'm twenty-one. I'll show you my birth certificate if you don't believe me..."

Without responding, the detective shouldered past him, followed by the other suited man and one of the police officers. Jake had been in too much of a flap, immediately after the sex, to take much notice of their faces. Now he recognised the officer who followed him back into back into the kitchen. It was Constable Jeff Collins.

"What the fuck are *you* doing here?" Jake asked him.

Jeff was in a flap, too. Grabbing Jake by the arm, he took him to one side.

"Do you think I *wanted* to come up here?" he whispered in Jake's ear. "Mark and I also had sex, remember, and quite a lot of it. Some of it in this very flat. *Please* don't say anything about what happened that afternoon in Mark's house. I'll lose my job if any of this gets out!"

Again, Jake asked what all this was about, but before Jeff could say any more the two detectives emerged from the bedroom, with Mark. He had on his trousers, but was still bare-chested...and he was handcuffed to the other policeman.

"I did it for you, baby," he told Jake. "Whatever happens to me, never forget that. Until the day I die, Jake Nelson, I'll never stop loving you..."

The burly officer turned towards Jeff, "Seeing as two of them were done on your patch, Constable Collins, I think you should do the honours."

Jeff stepped forwards and cleared his throat, and while Mark remained expressionless, the colour drained from Jake's face as he pronounced, "Mark Noble. I'm arresting you for the murders of Lennie Stevens, Edward Nelson and

194

Richard Ross. You don't have to say anything when questioned, but anything you do say may be taken down and used in evidence against you…"

Jake staggered, his whole life swimming before his eyes. Jeff had said *Richard Ross*. Ricky was *dead*…and Jeff was saying that Mark had killed him! He opened his mouth and tried to speak, but no words came out as the room started to spin. It was Jeff who caught him as he fell.

When Jake started to come to, a few minutes later, the others were gone—Mark, too. He had been installed in an armchair, and Jeff was sitting on a stool in front of him. It had all been a dream. He was back at Mark's cottage, and Ricky was in the kitchen fixing them something to eat after the wildest threesome ever. Why—Jeff had even put on his uniform to add authenticity to the proceedings! Then he blinked himself back to reality, as Jeff reached out and touched his hand.

"You're going to have to come with me to the station," he said. "We can do it here in Whitby, without you having to go all the way back home…"

"Home," Jake sighed, gazing into the big brown eyes. "I don't know where home is any more. My mother used to say it's where the heart is, but right now my heart feels like it's been ripped out."

Jeff wanted to envelop him in his arms, to take him into the room where they had just arrested Mark and make love to him, to tell him that everything was going to be all right. He squeezed Jake's hand so hard that his knuckles cracked.

"He was my lover, too, though obviously not as close to

195

me as he was to you," he said. "But if he says anything about that, I'll deny it and it'll be his word against mine. We have to do this, Jake, as soon as you're up to it. They've suspected Mark for some time, but they were waiting for all the evidence to come in before making an arrest. When I found out about it, it made me sick to the stomach. The last time I saw Ricky, we—"

"Fucked?" Jake finished for him. "How do you think I feel? We were living together...well, more or less."

He asked Jeff what had happened, and Jeff shook his head, "I'm not allowed to tell you, Jake. That's how it has to be for now. You'll know more after you've talked to CID. Meanwhile, is there anybody I can call? Somebody who can come and stay with you until this mess has been sorted out?"

Jake half-nodded, and numbly replied, "Justin, I guess. He was Davey Watson's other half. He must be feeling as rotten and alone as I do, right now..."

196

Epilogue

February-May 1965

Tommy Vincent had been interviewed by detectives, who had travelled down to London and asked him why Mark Noble had left the city under a darkened cloud, and headed for his sister's place up in Yorkshire. Much of what had actually transpired had been kept out of the papers, not just because of the savage nature of Mark's crimes, but because of his reasoning behind them—his obsession with a young man who, at the time the killings had taken place, had been under the age of consent. Tommy was reminded that homosexuality itself was a crime.

"I'm well aware of what the law dictates," Tommy had told the detective questioning him in a room which would not have gone amiss in a spy movie. "And you have proof that I've been involved with stuff like that, have you? What I might or might not do behind closed doors, or what you *think* I might do is nobody's business but my own whether it's with a male, a female, or Old Mother Riley's cat. So why don't you stick that in your pipe and smoke it?"

All the police learned from Tommy was that Mark had been employed by him as Lennie Stevens' driver, and that he had found the singer so loathsome that he had upped and left for Yorkshire without handing in his notice. The police wanted to know why Tommy had hired someone who lived two-hundred miles away to drive Lennie around, instead of a local man. Was this to take advantage of a gullible young man? Also, what was the "favour" that Tommy supposedly owed Mark, the one a distressed Jake had spoken about during questioning? Tommy had avowed that there had *been* no favour.

"Mark left because he couldn't stand Lenny," Tommy said in his statement. "Yes, it's true that I employed Jake when I could have got someone closer to home. The kid was Mark's friend and he was having family problems that I identified with. The original idea was for him to chauffeur one of my other acts—Tony Manila. Then Lennie's other chauffeur upped and left—his third in less than a year—so I gave him Jake, thinking that Lennie might not throw his weight around so much with a young man big enough to eat him alive. How wrong I was about that, though I figure Jake gave as good as he got, and Lennie actually got around to liking him. Was I involved with Jake other than in a boss-employee way? No, of course not, and I resent the implication that I might have been!"

"There are some things a man will take with him to the grave," Mark had said in his statement. "It's enough to say Lennie was treating Jake like shit—the way Jake's father had treated him like shit. He deserved better than that."

Wishing to rescue Jake from Lennie, his intention being to take him back to the cottage in Brodsworthy until such time as he had made arrangements for them to relocate to Whitby, Mark had headed for Liverpool.

"Every time Jake called, it was Lennie this, Lennie that. The bloke was making his life a misery. I knew it would be a matter of time before Jake snapped and turned on him, the way he had hit out at his father when Eddie went too far. In some ways I blamed Tommy Vincent for saddling him with such an arsehole in the first place. That wasn't the original idea. He and I had kept in touch since I moved up here to Yorkshire. I told him about Jake, about what had happened with his father and of how he was at a loss and staying with me until he'd worked out what to do next. 'Send him down here,' Tommy said. 'Tony Milano's chauffeur has just gone AWOL and I need somebody to fill in for a couple of weeks.' But instead of Tony, Jake ended up with Lennie. I knew from the first time Jake called that it would all end badly. And when Jake rang and said how he was dreading going on tour with him, I decided that I would have to get him out. So I drove to Liverpool…"

At Mark's trial, held in York in February 1965, the jury had been told that his plan had been to return Jake to his house in Brodsworthy, where they would live until relocating to Whitby—with Mark still denying that they had been more than just good friends. A hotel employee had spoken of witnessing an altercation between the accused and Lennie Stevens in a downstairs corridor in front of the cellar door when the singer had told Mark, "Jake doesn't want to go back with you. Last night, he and I made love for the first time, and it was wonderful!" The witness had not seen what had happened next—Mark dragging Lennie into the basement, knocking him out, and stringing him up with his belt, obviously to make it appear like suicide—save that Mark's fingerprints had been found everywhere.

Jake was called to the stand, during the trial. Like Mark,

he perjured himself by telling the jury that he and Mark had been just close friends—and added that at first he had considered it strange that Tommy Vincent should wish to hire him as a chauffeur.

"Mark told me how Tommy owed him a favour," he told the jury. "I didn't ask what this was because it was none of my business. Did Tommy try it on with me? No, he didn't."

Asked about his relationship with Ricky, while fighting to control the big lump that came to his throat, he said, "We met in a pub. I was in a strange place, feeling like a fish out of water. He was kind to me. When Lennie died he took me under his wing because the papers found out where I was staying and kept pestering me. When I came up here to get away from them, it seemed the right thing to do, asking him to come up here with me. I'll never forgive myself for that. It's because of me that he's dead. And you want to know if we were lovers? Yes, we were!"

Martha Longhurst brought unexpected hilarity to the proceedings when asked if she had ever suspected Lennie Stevens of having "inappropriate relations" with his young chauffeur—after John Paige, a porter at the Regency Hotel, had seen Lennie emerging from Jake's room wearing just a "cissy-looking" dressing-gown.

"Jake Nelson—a queer?" Martha had piped. "You must be joking. It took me over a week to come down from the clouds after what Jake did to me, that night!"

Mark Noble had been found guilty on two counts of murder—for killing Lennie and Eddie Nelson, the latter premeditated—and given two life-sentences. The judge told him that he was fortunate—of how, when he had presided over his last double-murder case, three years ago, the man found guilty had been sent to the gallows. He had however been cleared of killing Ricky, whose death had been ruled a tragic accident.

Fate, according to Mark in his statement to the police, had brought about Eddie Nelson's death. That evening, he had just left a friend's house in the village when he had seen Eddie staggering out of the pub, drunk as usual. He had followed him down the lane, past the cottage, and up the hill to the farm. Eddie had not seen him, even when he had followed him into the house and up the stairs. One little push and Eddie had gone arse-over-tit, slamming his head against the wall at the bottom. Mark had checked his pulse, and assured himself that Eddie was dead...only he had still been alive when the farmhand had found him.

"It was that pervert Mark Noble," he had managed to get out. "He said he's already done the singer, and that the Dilly Boy's going to be next, whoever he is..."

The farmhand had rung for an ambulance, and Eddie had died on his way to the hospital.

Jake had only found out what had really happened in that Liverpool hotel, and to Ricky, two weeks after the trial when Jeff Collins had come up to York, where Mark had been held since his arrest, to arrange for his transfer to Armley Prison, in Leeds. That same afternoon, he had driven up to Whitby to see how Jake was doing.

"Lennie was secretly queer, or at least he swung both ways," he had told Jake while sitting opposite him outside a pub overlooking the harbour, with both men wishing it might have been in more intimate surroundings. "All that talk of all the women he'd bedded, it was mostly in his head. Tommy Vincent shagged all his singers apart from Lennie. But Lennie kept taunting him—blowing kisses and mincing with his hands on his hips, that sort of thing. One minute he was telling Mark that all queers needed setting alight, the next he was making eyes at him. So he decided to teach him a lesson. Lennie was doing a show in Brighton, and he crept into his bedroom. Lennie was in the shower, so Mark got undressed and walked into the bathroom. Told him he was sick of his taunting—that he was going back to Yorkshire the next day, and that now was the time for Lennie to decide whether he was queer or not, or call security and have him thrown out. Lennie's response was to take him into the bedroom, where Mark fucked him."

Jake's eyes had opened wide at this, and his thoughts had returned to that night in Lennie's room when he had jokingly asked who wanted to be fucked first—him or Martha.

He had told Jeff, "Had I known he'd had his cock inside Lennie Stevens, I don't think I'd have wanted him to touch me again, no matter how many times he'd washed it..."

But, as Jeff had explained, there was more…

"Mark wasn't content with leaving things there. He began blackmailing Lennie. We think that's how he got the money to pay for the house. Well, some of it, because he'd already been left a fair amount by his father. We also think that Lennie would still be alive, if he hadn't boasted about having sex with you. Did you *really* fuck him, Jake, like he said? You can tell me. I swear it won't go any further…"

Jake had explained what had happened in Lennie's room —how he had shot his load across Lennie's face—and Jeff had roared with laughter, so much so that the other drinkers sitting nearby had paused to stare. Mirth had turned to tears, however, when Jeff had told him about Ricky.

Inasmuch as Mark had headed for Liverpool to rescue Jake from Lennie Stevens, so he had driven to Brodsworthy in the hope of wooing him away from Ricky. And as had happened with Eddie Nelson, Fate had intervened.

Jeff had explained, "He parked his car in the pub yard, as usual, and was walking down the lane when he saw you, up on the top of the hill on the way to the farm, he guessed for your dad's funeral. He was about to shout to you when he saw Ricky coming out of the house. In his statement he said that Ricky stopped to have a pee halfway up the hill, and that's when he caught up with him. He said that Ricky turned around fast, slipped and hit his head on the dry-stone wall. Forensics found blood there, it's true. But if that's what happened, why didn't he just call somebody instead of dragging his body away and going back later to bury it? Why did he go back to the house and write that goodbye note, letting you think it was from Ricky? Accident or not, the judge at the next hearing gave him another five years. By my reckoning, he'll be over seventy when he comes out of prison—that's *if* he comes out."

*

203

Jake's ordeal was over. His name was on the rent-book for the flat in Whitby. The day after Mark's arrest, he had thrown out the bed that they had slept and made love in and bought a new one. He had even replaced the sink he had shot his load in, that morning while the police had been walking down the path. The money had come through from the sale of the farm. Justin had gone halves with him, after selling the house he had lived in with Davey Watson, and they had paid cash-in-hand for a little terrace house in town. Justin had also successfully applied for a teaching position at a local grammar school. The driver who had left Davey dead at the side of the road had been caught, and ironically was serving five years for manslaughter in the same prison as Mark.

Turning on to his side, Jake studied the profile of the man sleeping next to him, and realised how lucky he was. Justin had helped him through his breakdown—he, the tough-as-nails farmer's boy who for a while had genuinely believed he had been going off his head. He, who had always believed that psychiatrists were only for nut-cases, had submitted to seeing one at the local hospital. She had talked him through each stage of his trauma, and taught him how to live with and control his demons. There were occasions when he had nightmares, days when he would suddenly go to pieces, but these "episodes" were getting less frequent. He was on the mend.

Jake found Justin's profile exquisite, like that of a Greek god. Then he spoke, scarcely moving his lips, proving that he was not asleep at all.

"Are you having mucky thoughts about me, Mr. Nelson? Are you hard?"

"I'm always having mucky thoughts about you, Mr. Banks," he chuckled. "As for the other, see for yourself…"

With one movement, he kicked the sheets off the bed, and sighed contentedly as Justin rolled on top of him and they kissed.

Printed in Great Britain
by Amazon

61867197R00117